ULTIMATE PURPOSE

ULTIMATE PURPOSE

SARAH RUTH SCOTT

authorHOUSE®

AuthorHouse™ UK Ltd.
1663 Liberty Drive
Bloomington, IN 47403 USA
www.authorhouse.co.uk
Phone: 0800.197.4150

© *2014 Sarah Ruth Scott. All rights reserved.*

No part of this book may be reproduced, stored in a retrieval system, or transmitted by any means without the written permission of the author.

Published by AuthorHouse   05/05/2014

ISBN: 978-1-4969-7973-5 (sc)
ISBN: 978-1-4969-7975-9 (e)

Any people depicted in stock imagery provided by Thinkstock are models, and such images are being used for illustrative purposes only. Certain stock imagery © Thinkstock.

This book is printed on acid-free paper.

Because of the dynamic nature of the Internet, any web addresses or links contained in this book may have changed since publication and may no longer be valid. The views expressed in this work are solely those of the author and do not necessarily reflect the views of the publisher, and the publisher hereby disclaims any responsibility for them.

Cover design portrait of Siena from 'Blood trail' by Stephen Robert Sutton
Art work and design by Stephen and Michael Sutton.
With a special thank you to my editor Rachel Day

TABLE OF CONTENTS

1. BLOOD TRAIL 1
   Introduction 1
   The Blood Trail Begins 1
   Into The Darkness 14
   Laura The Witch 26
   The Lost Poet 32
   A King Without A Kingdom 33
   The Evil Count Vermont 39

2. CRACKED PORCELAIN 43
   Broken Wings And Lost Souls 43

3. ALL ABOUT FAITH -
   UNDERSTANDING JODIE 84
   Reflecting Back 87
   Oh To Be A Goth 108

These stories were written in two of my favourite haunts the Causeway Café and the Coffee House both in Lichfield, other books were written in various locations in Manchester and even as far as Sweden and United states of America. I wrote some of my work such as 'Cracked porcelain' at Hawksyard Priory Nursing Home when I was off duty of course!

ACKNOWLEDGEMENTS

Thank you to everyone concerned with the compiling and inspiration of this book, some characters are actually from real people I know and love. May you now be immortalised in this work especially those at my present employment. May I say a special thank you to my friends in Sweden and the United States. I wish to thank my parents for giving me the gift of art and writing.

With a special mention to Rachel Day for her help and to Jennifer Sutton for her guidance.

A special mention to Michael Sutton for his valuable input.

ULTIMATE PURPOSE

This book is a collection of stories, which are fictitious, however like stories Beyond Belief book one, some of the characters are real and some situations can be believable. I will leave it to your own imagination which parts are factual and where I got most of the characters for my books, needless to say a lot of people I have either worked with or met over the years. The idea of 'Blood Trail' is to follow the life of a vampire who desires to be human again, after years of taking blood to survive she asks God to help her become a human and live a normal life once more. To achieve this she has to accomplish tasks and defeat the vampire that made her a vampire.

The next story called Cracked Porcelain—Broken Wing and Lost Souls' follows the career and life of a psychiatric nurse called Ruth, her journey of life involves being involved with a murderous psychopath and finding her own comfort zone after childhood abuse. She is also discovering her own sexuality in an ever changing world where same sex relationships are just being excepted, with this and the shock of her friend Kathy discovering that she has cancer. Amidst all the dilemma her dead girl friend Pamela lurks in the shadows as a ghost watching over Ruth.

The third story is about a guardian angel called Faith who in her efforts, helps a number of people in their life to survive many problems. Faith has to learn to understand humans in order to help them and so she lives amongst them for a while. But her adversary Dawn attempts to prevent from helping people and causes her harm, she eventually destroys Dawn and her wicked demons and is attacked by her sister Sonia in a desperate attempt to take over the earth. Now after the failed efforts to invade the earth, the demons try a more subtle approach to conquering the earth with a more intense style of evil warfare. Fiona is the latest demon to be sent to a prison to capture souls and recruit an army of demons that will rule the earth. A girl called Jodie has been chosen as the main target, she is in prison for murder and considered ideal to join Satan's army. Faith has to enter the prison in order to save her and prove that she can be a true guardian angel.

BLOOD TRAIL

INTRODUCTION

A woman called Siena enters the future through a picture and befriends a man Jack who later discovers he is in love with a vampire. However this is just the beginning of his problems as vampire slayers also enter the future and both are faced with more than they bargain for in this fast pace story of romance and intrigue. The story takes the readers through a journey through time meeting interesting characters and danger around every corner. Siena wants to be human again and asks God to help her reach her goal, a guardian angel called Faith appears with a mission to defeat the vampire that cursed her life in order to be human again she persuades Jack and others to help her achieve this.

THE BLOOD TRAIL BEGINS

It was a cold night, the moon was full and the trees blew wildly in the air, in the thick of the forest a woman ran frantically for her life. She had mud on her pale face and torn clothes, she had fear in her green eyes and constantly looked back holding back her hood in order to see her pursuers. She could hear them shouting and holding clubs, the loud snapping of twigs suggested they were getting closer. Suddenly she caught her arm on a branch scratching the flesh on her wrist it began to bleed and she fell over another branch down a ditch. Her eyes started to blur as she desperately tried to get to her feet, she noticed a castle in the clearing and began to run towards it. She was followed by two of the men, who began to run behind her, she arrived at the main door, which was open and proceeded down a long corridor. She appeared to know where she was going and entered a room; blood began to trickle down her arm as she gazed at a portrait painting of a man. She noticed a strange thing about the painting as the man in the portrait began to look as if he was moving and the background appeared transparent. She put her hand on the picture and her hand seemed to blend into it, so she withdrew her hand in shock, then out of curiosity she placed her hand in a little further. At that moment she heard voices and noticing the blood dripping from her fingers put the rest of her body through the picture. She found herself rushing through some kind of wind tunnel with swirls of light travelling around her pushing her forward leading through another picture. She eventually reached the other end of her journey and landed onto the floor on top of a man.

After wrestling with him, she managed to break free and he stood to his feet and offered a hand to help her to her feet. She slapped his hand and managed to stand by herself looking very annoyed by his actions.

"Get off me and stay away from me," she shouted.

"Hey calm down," he replied looking around him.

"How did you get on me like that?" she asked.

"Well I was admiring that picture," he pointed to the picture. "When you shot out of it and fell on top of me."

"Oh you mean that picture I feel really odd," she said holding her head.

"What's wrong?" he said touching her on the arm.

"Don't touch me," she said nervously "I warn you I bite."

"I am not going to harm you, I just want to help," he insisted.

"So who are you and where am I?" She asked.

"I am Jack Clarke and this is an art gallery," Jack said. "Don't you know where you are?" he said bewildered by her strange manner.

"I am Siena, I was being chased in a forest and ran into a castle, a weird thing happened, I seemed to enter a picture and landed here." Siena explained.

"Wherever here is?" she said looking round the room with her green eyes.

"Come let's get some air," Jack said leading Siena to the exit.

Suddenly Siena saw daylight and froze like a statue by the door.

"I think I will stay inside for a while," Siena said shaking.

"Ok let's get a drink in the canteen," Jack suggested.

"That sounds good to me," Siena said relieved.

They walked towards the canteen passing art displays such as pictures, statues and other strange shaped objects. Siena was bewildered by the displays and appeared disorientated by her surroundings. The clothes that people were wearing also fascinated her; she continued to hold her head sitting at a table.

"So who was chasing you?" Jack asked.

"Oh a few strange men with clubs annoyed about something," Siena said avoiding eye contact.

"Oh that explains a lot," Jack said sarcastically.

"Look I have to get back," Siena said worried.

"But your in danger there," Jack said concerned.

"I am not safe here either, I can't explain it but believe me I am," Siena said trembling.

"Listen! You don't recognise objects and outside scares you so I can only conclude that you are from the past and that you entered some sort of time portal," Jack said. "I can't think of any other explanation."

"You're speaking nonsense I only know I have to return home," Siena insisted.

"Well we need to get back to the picture," Jack explained. "There lies the answer to problems you have been facing."

They finished their drinks and went back to the area where the picture was being displayed. No one was in the area and the gallery was about to close Siena saw the picture but it didn't seem the same, she went to touch it placing her hand on the canvas but nothing happened. She tried again and suddenly heard shouting from a distance as a guard approached them.

"Don't touch the paintings they are valuable," the guard said.

"Sorry," Jack said. "I was examining the texture."

"What do I do now?" Siena asked. "I am stuck here."

"I have an idea," Jack said leading her back to the exit.

It was dark outside but it was very busy with a lot of traffic, Jack hailed a taxi and gave the driver his address. When they entered the taxi Siena began to stare at him, she had not really realised how handsome he was with his blue eyes and fair hair, he was clean-shaven and had a prominent chin. He was looking back at her trying to see beyond a dirty face and frowning expression she had removed her hood revealing her long black hair and unusual fringe. She was suddenly startled by a car horn and jumped, then the sound of ambulance sirens, which raced past her window at great speed. She clung hold of Jacks arm and he could feel the tension in her fingers as they dug into him like a claw.

"You're quite safe Siena believe me," Jack said reassuringly.

"I wish I could believe that," Siena said staring out into the streets fascinated by the neon lights, which lit up the area around them.

Jack could feel Siena's heart beating next to him as she drew ever closer to his side, he put his arm around her to reassure her and she began to relax.

They finally reached their destination the taxi stopped outside his apartment, Jack paid the fare and they walked out into the cold dark street. Jack escorted Siena to the apartment block and tried to enter discreetly, unfortunately he was stopped by a friend.

Pier was a French friend who had spent a lot of time with Jack during his college days, he was dark skinned and smelt of garlic as Siena was introduced to him she ran into the building. Siena had also noticed a crucifix around his neck, Pier was a catholic and usually wore rosary. But he had left France with a little cynicism in mind, his exposure to the wider world made him think that the increased presence of evil was more than enough reason to doubt the existence of any God. The people that professed to be good such as priests and nuns appeared to have a bad reputation, the exposure of child abuse or forms of fornication turned a lot of people against them. Jack said goodbye to Pier and walked over to a frightened Siena, He never spoke to her but led her into his apartment.

Siena looked around the room then began to yawn and lay on the settee, she soon drifted off to sleep. Jack found a blanket and placed it over her, he then took the phone off the receiver so that she would not be disturbed. He sat close by admiring her beautiful face; he couldn't help feeling that there was more to her than she admitted. He reflected back on his first encounter of her as she jumped out of the picture, from the time portal and falling onto him.

Once she had woken up Jack showed her how to operate the shower then left her to wash herself in private. She couldn't believe the way the shower worked, letting the water flow down upon he. He had pointed out the shower gel and shampoo and she seemed to be in the shower for a long time. When she came out she was wearing Jacks bathrobe, Jack had washed her clothes and sat watching television. But Siena noticed that he was watching a vampire movie called Van Helsing a vampire slayer. She seemed disturbed by the television alone but worse by the sight of someone killing vampires.

"Oh Siena, was everything alright?" Jack asked concerned.

"Yes I feel a little better now," Siena said smiling.

"Let me turn this rubbish off, vampires as if they exist," Jack said turning off the television.

"If you say so," Siena said sitting on the settee.

Jack dealt with Siena's wounded arm using a bowl of warm water, antiseptic and a clean towel.

"This wound needs attention, you really need to go to hospital," Jack advised.

"No not that, I will be ok," Siena replied.

"But you look pale, you must have lost a lot of blood?" Jack said concerned.

"I said I am alright, it's nothing I have had worse," Siena said bluntly.

"Then let me dress it," Jack said opening a dressing pack. "My ex girlfriend used to be a nurse," Jack explained.

"I see, well I am honestly alright so just dress it please," Siena insisted.

Jack finished cleaning and dressing her arm and then put the remainder of the first aid kit away in the cupboard and returned to sit beside Siena.

Siena kept yawning and nodding off to sleep with her legs elevated and her head on the arm of the chair, she looked so fresh and clean, with her hair shining and flowing down with her soft pale skin gleaming. Jack was admiring her as she slept; she had just come into his life and he considered himself very lucky to have her in his home. He was hoping that they would get together as a couple but he was not lucky with women and he had the feeling that she would suddenly disappear probably back through the time portal.

Siena awoke again and looked across at Jack her eyes were glazed and she seemed pale as if she was suffering from anaemia.

"Can I offer you food and a drink?" Jack said concerned.

"Yes please," Siena said politely.

Jack went into the kitchen and returned with sandwiches, cut and placed neatly on a plate, went back out and returned with two mugs of tea with sugar and milk. She put two heaped spoonfuls of sugar in her mug and a tiny drop of milk, she stirred it slowly and took a sip from the mug. They had a brief conversation about Jacks job in a hospital kitchen just around the corner. Then Siena explained about the place she lived in, but seemed to be holding a lot of information back particularly about her family.

That night Jack offered to sleep on the settee while Siena slept on the bed, Siena reluctantly accepted. That night the moon was full and the sky was clear and full of stars Siena looked out through the window watching the wind blowing the trees. Siena opened the window and then crept towards the door and watched Jack sleeping she then returned to the window and jumped out onto a tree and down to the street. She came to an alley where a woman was walking alone, suddenly she was joined by two men as they got closer one of them grabbed her the other man then spoke to her.

"Now just do as we say and you wont get hurt," he said in a deep gravely voice.

She began to struggle and scream so one of the men slapped her knocking her to the ground. The other began to pull down his trousers while the other man held her; she continued to struggle as he attempted to remove her clothes.

Siena raced forward and knocked the man over with his trousers down his ankles, she had changed into a vampire and seemed to have incredible strength. She hit the other man and knocked him into a wall, he fell down the brickwork with his head bleeding.

"Go run away," Siena said but the woman didn't need telling she ran from the alley with great speed.

Siena walked back to the man who was conscious and pulling up his trousers, she grabbed him and held him tightly. Her eyes seemed to hypnotise him, while she began to caress him around his genitals.

"Let's make love," Siena said smiling.

"Wow ok," he replied excitedly.

Siena kissed his neck and then pierced his skin with her fangs and began sucking the blood from his body until he was drained of life and his limp body fell to the ground. She then walked over to the unconscious man and did the same to him, sucked his blood and left him dead in the alley.

Siena had begun to feel better and wandered back to the apartment entering it via the window as she did earlier. She got undressed and settled into bed feeling that she could rest comfortably knowing that she had received her life sustenance, human blood.

The next morning Siena was fast asleep and Jack was in the shower, he had switched on the television and the news was on. The two bodies discovered in the alley were the main feature, but also Pier had been murdered in the same way.

The question was did Siena murder Pier because he two had two puncture marks in the neck, in the same way that Siena had killed the two men. The news report repeated throughout the day, Jack saw it later as he returned from work that day. He avoided disturbing Siena knowing that she needed the rest.

He looked in on her sleeping soundly, lying across the bed with her head facing away from the window.

Siena sat beside Jack listening to him as he discussed the murders; she had tried to show no emotion as he went into graphic detail. She wanted to forget the experience and knew that she would venture out for yet another night, seeking out victims in order to obtain their blood and live another day.

Jack noticed that she seemed disturbed and sat closer to her, she glanced at him and smiled leaning on his arm and resting her head on his shoulder.

"You are very kind to me and a real gentleman," Siena said smiling.

"I know how to respect women and as you have come from another time you are naturally bewildered by what you see and hear," Jack explained.

"But you can teach me and show me your world?" Siena said looking into his eyes.

"Yes I can but so much has changed since your time, cars, planes and telephones," Jack said trying to imagine what she was thinking.

"Inventions and scary machines that are so noisy" Siena had not taken her eyes off Jack, she began to feel a tingle down her spine and the hair stood up at the back of her neck.

Jack drew ever closer to her, looking into her green eyes and feeling strange in her presence. It was like something he had never felt before, and began to relax he began to drift off to sleep. At this point Siena began to kiss him on the lips and his neck, then she suddenly changed and her fangs appeared. She leapt off the settee and onto the floor, she had realised what she had done by hypnotising Jack and trying to bite his neck, fortunately she managed to stop herself in time.

Jack awoke from his trance and saw Siena sat on the floor; she had a suspicious look on her face and appeared nervous.

"What has just happened to me?" Jack asked her.

"I think you fainted," Siena said in response. "You were sat with me and made me jump when you suddenly woke up."

Jack seemed to accept her explanation and never mentioned the situation again. Siena was more aware of her actions after this time and the next time they were close was not due to her but Jack who made advances to her. Jack had been going out to work during the day and with Siena at night, Siena continued to sneak out and find her own blood bank choosing people who were in her eyes wicked or deviant souls. This was her justification for taking and draining their blood, ending their life the only way a vampire knows feeding off humans and surviving leaving a blood trail.

Jack cuddled up to Siena and put his arm around her, Siena felt uneasy, as she was afraid of what she might do to him. Jack began to kiss her on the lips and she felt her heart begin to beat faster, her desire for him had become too great to resist and she kissed him back. A rush of passion overcome them both and they were soon in the throws of making love, items of clothing were removed they were both wild as they seemed to tear at each others clothes until they were naked. They headed for the bedroom and continued making love, neither relented as they went from the bedroom into the shower. Their naked flesh became entwined as the water from the shower trickled gently down their bodies and the steam from the water misted the glass cubical.

The months passed by and they lived the same way with Jack working at the hospital and coming home to a special lady and Siena at home cleaning the apartment and cooking delicious meals. Life seemed perfect for a while, but Siena continued to sleep part of the day and went out at night for her usual feast. Pierre was walking past the forest when he heard a female voice coming from the trees, he followed the voice into the thick of the forest. When he stopped he was met by a woman who he couldn't see properly, she managed to hypnotise him before attacking him sinking her fangs into his neck and draining the blood from him. It was like being attacked by a savage animal. The vampire had to survive and the blood was keeping her alive, however what Siena failed to realise was that she was not alone, the time portal had invited others through and Tom the vampire slayer had followed her along with others namely vampires.

Siena walked through the woods, she reached a stream and crossed an old wooden bridge that she recognised from her past. She looked down into the stream and saw her mother's face in the water as if she was really there.

"Mother help me, show me the way I am so lost, I want Jack to live with me forever, I don't want to live alone as a vampire, living off other humans".

"My child I died here as you know, killed by slayers, you must choose your own course I miss you too", She said then faded away.

"Mother don't go please" Siena pleaded but her mother was gone.

INTO THE DARKNESS

Yet again it was a full moon Siena lay beside Jack she was feeling particularly weak and looked very pale, she looked at Jacks naked neck and suddenly her fangs appeared and her eyes became wild staring at her victims flesh. As she approached him slowly and breathed cold air on his neck, he suddenly awoke and turned his head towards her. Then looked in horror as she was still trying to bite his neck and suck his blood.

"Oh my god!" Jack shouted. "You're a vampire, you are actually a vampire!"

Jack pushed her away and she fell off the bed, she tried to get up but Jack pointed to her angrily and she stayed on the floor.

"I have been sleeping with a vampire, its all coming clear to me now, Pier had eaten garlic and he had a crucifix did you kill him?"

"No I didn't," Siena said starting to change back to human form. "But then other vampires could have travelled through the picture as I did."

"And what about that vampire movie, you knew you were a vampire when we were watching it and said nothing?" Jack began shaking his head. "You were going to bite me and drain me of my blood."

"I know I'm sorry," Siena said with her head bowed. "I wanted you to be like me and live forever."

"Oh I see, you're sorry! That helps until I sleep again and you actually bite me," Jack said upset.

"For god sake I didn't plan to be a vampire, I didn't wake one morning and say I want to be a vampire or seek Count Vermont and say make me a vampire!" Siena said angrily.

"So how did it happen?" Jack asked.

"I was walking in the woods one night when I heard the breaking of branches I ran further in to the wood and came out in a clearing. I began to run and was suddenly surrounded by bats that turned into vampires; two of them grabbed me and took me to the Castle Vermont where I met the Count. He put me in some kind of trance and then bit my neck draining my blood, then he did a very odd thing he sent blood back into my body which brought me back from death making me a vampire. I then had to rely on him to keep me alive showing me how to take blood and survive in my present state, he even changed my name from Charlotte to Siena." Siena explained.

"That's quite a story," Jack said astonished.

"You don't believe me?" Siena said sadly.

"Yes I do. But I must confess it's a lot to take in and we need to get help for you," Jack said concerned.

"Who is going to help a blood sucking vampire?" Siena said.

"Have you tried asking God?" Jack said confident that he had the answer to her dilemma.

"God? He helps good people not people like me," Siena became tearful.

"Why don't you go to church and ask him, he is merciful and kind," Jack said trying to reason with her.

"If I enter the house of God I will die, I cannot even enter the doorway," Siena said becoming agitated

"Stop! My theory is this, if you are to be helped then you will be protected. God will see the sincerity in your heart and help you," Jack felt that his explanation was enough to convince her to enter the church.

"Well what have I got to lose? I could risk being destroyed in church or by Tom the vampire slayer," Siena thought for a moment. "Alright I will do it".

That evening Siena entered the graveyard and began walking up the pathway towards the church, suddenly she was startled by the voice of a woman.

"Are you going somewhere Siena?" came the voice.

Siena turned around and saw a blonde haired woman floating above her head, when she turned back two other women with darker hair stood in front of her. "We have been searching for you," one of them said.

"Yes you have been hiding from us," said the other.

"I stumbled into this picture and found myself here," Siena said trying to get past them.

"My dear you must come with us to the master," one of them said blocking her way.

"Yes the master is angry with you, you have disappointed him," one of the others said also blocking her way.

"Come let's go," the blonde woman said.

During the scuffle an arrow was fired into the air and hit the blonde woman in the chest, she immediately disintegrated. This was followed by another arrow that hit one of the others who also became dust. Siena ducked behind a gravestone and the other woman flew away narrowly dodging arrows, eventually she too was destroyed.

Siena entered the church aware that Tom the slayer was watching her from a distance, but she was hoping that he wouldn't follow her. He seemed surprised that she was entering a church and stopped by a tree waiting for her to reappear. But Siena walked towards the altar and tried to look at the cross in front of her, she reverted her eyes at the statue of Mary holding Jesus in her arms. Tears filled her eyes and she fell to her knees, she then sobbed for a while then began speaking in a low voice.

"God please help me I know that I have done bad things and even caused deaths, I am cursed as a vampire and want to be human again," Siena paused and looked through the gaps in her fingers. "I haven't disintegrated so I presume that you have heard my prayer and are considering it?"

At that moment she heard a voice coming from behind her.

"Siena," came the female voice.

Siena turned to see an image appear it was an angel wearing a white dress and carrying a key, which was tied to a sash and hung down from her neck to her thigh.

"I am Faith, I am a guardian angel and have a message from God," Faith said sincerely.

"An angel but why are you here are you going to kill me?" Siena said concerned.

"No. I am here to help you, God is merciful and wants to help you, if you are prepared to help yourself, are you willing to do this?" Faith asked.

"Yes of course, so what do I do?" Siena said eagerly.

"Then you must perform a number of tasks to prove yourself worthy," Faith continued. "You need to go back in time to where you became a vampire, you then need to collect a series of objects and take them to the Castle Vermont the final object is worn by Count Vermont and this is a pendant to take this from him he must die and you will rid the land of evil." Faith said.

"So what about these other objects, where do I find them?" Siena asked.

"One will lead to another and each one will introduce you to someone who needs help and you will provide that help." Faith explained.

"But what about me wont I need help?" Siena asked.

"You must promise not to take blood from others and not kill anyone but the evil ones, you will be helped but you must have Faith in God." Faith said touching her wrist.

"But I am a vampire I take blood because I would die without it," Siena said concerned.

"Look at your wrist Siena," Faith said pointing to a shining bracelet.

"What's this?" Siena asked.

"This will prevent you from taking blood and keep you alive, never remove it this will protect you," Faith explained. "Try to divert your mind from evil thoughts."

"Thank you. Can Jack come with me?" Siena asked.

"It has already been arranged, my friend Harmony has visited him," Faith said. "May God bless you and have a safe journey," with those words Faith vanished.

At that moment Tom the slayer entered the church and ran towards her, he knocked her to the ground and pulled a stake from his bag. Siena held her arm up in order to protect her and it shone into Toms eyes, he yelled out and dropped the stake and scrambled to find it.

At that moment Jack entered the church, he ran up to Tom and disarmed him.

"Siena I was visited by an angel called Harmony and she told me what I need to do in order to help you. She told me everything about you becoming human and what is required, I am coming with you, I want to help you."

"You have helped me Jack," Siena insisted.

"I know but I don't want to lose you," Jack said holding her.

"Come with me because I feel the same, I want you close by my side," Siena said.

"Tom we need your help in order to find Count Vermont, are you with us?" jack asked.

"Tom help me become human again, let's destroy the evil that has cursed our people?" Siena said pleading with him.

"I am with you what do we do?" Tom asked.

"Go to the gallery and enter the time portal?" Jack suggested.

"Exactly we must return home Tom," Siena said.

"I am ready to face the evil of the dark world," Tom said positively.

The three arrived at the gallery hoping to find the time portal; they searched for the picture that Jack would recognise, to his delight the portrait of a lady appeared. But it seemed just like the other paintings stunning and attractive, with nothing special to tell them that this was a time portal. It had no depth and looked nothing like the painting that Siena had came from and fell on Jack. Desperately they waited for the picture to change; meanwhile the security guards were ushering people out of the gallery. One guard approached them looking very official and determined to close the gallery on time.

"We are about to close," he said in a stern manner.

"Can I ask you something about this painting?" Jack said diverting him away from the others.

"Yes of course, it was imported from Germany, it was originally the property of Count Vermont said to have been a vampire," the security officer said pleased to provide Jack with the information. "The painting is said to be enchanted and holds many secrets, obviously this is ridiculous just like the legend of vampires."

"Of course," Jack replied watching Siena and Tom vanish into the picture behind the guard.

Siena landed in the same room where she began her journey through time, she looked at the portrait watching Tom appear. It seemed a long time before Jack arrived he fell to the ground and seemed dazed lying on the floor, both Siena and Tom helped him up.

"Welcome to Fort David," Siena said.

"So this is it, the castle where you came from" Jack said holding his head.

"Are you alright?" Tom asked.

"Yes. I had to lose the guard before following you, he took some losing believe me,".Jack said looking back at the picture.

"I think we ought to go before anyone sees us," Tom said opening the door and stepping into the corridor.

They walked outside looking for the right direction to find the giant Fargo who would help them find Laura the witch.

Fargo was not difficult to find, sitting on a rock he was an eight-foot man with a brown beard, muscular body with long hair tied back in a pony tail. He had a fat broken nose and a scar on his chin, he appeared to have been involved in battle previously.

They approached Fargo confident that he would greet them with open arms and willingly help them. But the giant seemed hostile and defensive and resented Siena being there and wanting his help, he didn't trust her suspecting that she might lead them into a trap when they arrived at Castle Vermont if not before.

"You must be Fargo?" Siena said offering to shake his hand.

"I am," Said Fargo refusing to shake her hand. "I have something for you."

"A red stone, perhaps a ruby?" Siena said realising that he didn't trust her.

"Yes a ruby representing the blood of Vermont," Fargo said looking at the other two men.

"Oh yes, this is Jack and Tom they are helping us," Siena said.

"We travel tomorrow. You can stay in my cave behind those trees," Fargo said.

"It is surrounded by garlic to ward away the vampires," Fargo looked at Siena and back at the trees covering the cave. "But how will you enter the cave?"

"I have a protective bracelet which is helping me to survive at present," Siena explained. "Providing I do good I will be protected."

"Then its up to you to avoid evil and follow to path to goodness," Fargo said sincerely.

"Yes I must, I know this," Siena said.

They entered the cave and Fargo found an area for them to sleep, the cave was well lit with burning torches every few yards. The walls were decorated with paintings of birds and wild animals; a book lay on a table near by written on the cover were the words 'Best Poems'. The floor seemed gritty and elements of sand were present indicating the presence of the coast, like a sandy beach.

"Are you hungry?" Fargo asked.

"A little," Jack admitted.

"Then lets feast my friends," Fargo said uncovering food on a table.

Siena didn't eat much and became very pale and looking very tired.

"I think I will just rest if you don't mind?" Siena said walking towards the bedded area.

Fargo watched her leave the area and looked at the others in disbelief.

"I don't trust her, she may be protected but she's still a vampire," Fargo said.

"She's okay. I have been with her for a while and I was safe," Jack said looking at them both.

They spoke for a while then settled to bed, but during the night Siena was approached and the person concerned had a stake in his hand. He pressed it against her chest and attempted to hammer it into her chest with a wooden mallet. Suddenly Jack jumped in the way and almost got injured from the stake that hit him in the side.

"Fargo stop!" Tom shouted. "Trust us she is of no danger to you."

"You maniac you nearly killed her!" Jack said with his side bleeding.

Siena hugged him then saw the blood. "Help him Tom please."

Siena then turned to Fargo and spoke to him. "Fargo let me tell you something, I have come here to defeat evil, to change my life and with the will of God become human again," Siena said angrily.

"I will not try to harm you again, I promise," Fargo said ashamed of himself.

"I want to be your friend and for us all to work together and destroy Vermont and his vampires," Siena said putting her hand out in friendship.

Fargo shuck her by the hand "I am sorry," he said sincerely.

"It's alright now, lets help Jack," Siena said going back to Jack.

"He is fine the stake just caught the skin," Tom explained.

They all rested and the next morning Tom asked for weapons to protect themselves from Count Vermont's followers. Fargo showed them weapons, crossbows with deadly arrows powerful enough to kill the enemy.

"Crossbows and other weapons," Fargo said.

"A complete arsenal for us all," Tom said happily.

"Well don't miss and hit me," Siena said jokingly.

"I will watch out for you Siena, after all you have to kill Count Vermont."

They then went in search of Laura the white witch; Fargo knew exactly where to find her and seemed happy to lead the way.

LAURA THE WITCH

They saw the cave amongst the trees and bushes; they followed a small path towards it. Once inside they were taken by surprise as they saw all kinds of treasures collected from various places that Laura had visited. To say she was a witch she was not the type that Jack had read about for he imagined a cauldron, possibly a broomstick and dolls that would simulate someone she despised with pins in them.

"This is no witches place," Jack said almost disappointed.

"Not all witches are dark and sinister, some are good witches," Siena said.

"I have never heard of a good witch," Jack said confused.

"Perhaps we should go?" Fargo said concerned.

At that moment Laura appeared with her golden hair and long pastel coloured dress, she had blue eyes and her long hair was plaited and shaped, she looked as if she had a tiara on her head. She seemed to swoop down to them from above and was displeased at their presence.

"Who are you and why have you entered my home uninvited?" Laura asked.

"I am Siena. I have been sent to you from the future, a guardian angel Faith sent me to you," Siena explained.

"Then you are the one who is going to rid this world of evil?" Laura said.

"Yes I guess I am Laura," Siena said confidently.

"I have something for you," Laura looked in a treasure chest and produced a bracelet for her other wrist, which she put on her and kissed it.

"This will protect you from the vampires and from evil," Laura said. "But never remove it until the evil has been destroyed."

"Are you not going to travel with us?" Siena asked.

"No. But I will be observing you and be with you in spirit," Laura said.

"So which way now?" Jack asked.

"The home of Lilly the child?" Tom said.

"Yes, she is just over that hill my dear," Laura said pointing outside the cave.

"Thank you Laura," Siena said.

"Good luck. I hope you do well," Laura said smiling.

Siena couldn't help admitting that she was disappointed that Laura would not be with them, if for nothing else she could have provided her with moral support and female companionship. But Laura had her own reasons not to join them and was reluctant to share them with Siena or her friends.

So Siena and her companions continued on their arduous journey travelling over the hillside in search of Lilly who was running around a garden beside an old cottage. She saw Siena and smiled sweetly at her standing still near a tree, her face was very round and she had a lovely smile, her ginger hair was long and curly which suited her blue eyes and pale complexion.

"Hello," she said sweetly. "I am Lilly," Lilly said politely.

"I am Siena," Siena replied. "This is Jack, Tom and Fargo."

"I have something for you Siena," Lilly said running into the house.

She returned with a ring.

"This belonged to my mother who was killed by vampires a while ago, you must put it on your finger," Lilly explained. "It will guide you to the Castle Vermont."

"Thank you Lilly. Are you joining us?" Siena asked.

"No she can't. It's too dangerous," Tom said.

"I am coming, please Siena I won't be any trouble and I can help cook for you" Lilly said.

"I want her with me," Siena insisted.

"Well you will have to protect her yourself," Tom said.

"I don't mind. Get your things together Lilly," Siena said. "I will come in the house with you," Siena said holding her hand and leading her inside.

Inside the cottage the furniture was mostly made of wood and at back of the cottage was a small but quaint kitchen. Lilly led Siena up the stairs, she took her into a small room and took a small rucksack and put a few items of clothes in it. Then she took a small cuddly bear and stuffed it in as deep as she could so that only the head was showing.

"I am ready," Lilly said smiling and placing a small book in her bag.

"Listen Lilly it is going to be dangerous, I wouldn't like anything to happen to you. Don't you have any family?" Siena asked concerned.

"No one at all. I have had to live alone," Lilly said. "My book keeps me company."

"Very well, let's go Lilly," Siena said leading the way down the stairs and outside to join the others.

They walked across a bridge entering a forest, Siena was curious to know what was written in the book that fascinated Lilly but she never asked.

They camped in the forest overnight Lilly began to sing like a nightingale, her voice was soft and melodic they all listened to her intently. They all had supper and discussed their journey. Then Lilly began to read her book out loud.

"The poet writes his final line about things that couldn't be, he lives his life in solitude with things you cannot see. Hidden away in a fortress tower so high upon a hill, lost within his solitude with dreams he could not fulfil." Lilly paused to observe her audiences reaction then continued. "A trapped talent within a cell within his mind fresh thoughts do dwell, a man that is trapped within his mind, here the Lost Poet may dwell. Always thinking about the people you create, when you're asleep fresh thoughts you motivate. Like a person within a person or fictitious people within a dream and nightmares make you awake and no one will here you scream."

"That's really intense," Jack said looking at the others.

"Is that from your own mind?" Siena asked.

"It came to me," Lilly said turning the page. "May I read on?"

"Of course," Fargo said smiling. "Tell us more."

"So daylight is over and darkness will end the day, the candles burn so low and just as the hot sun melts the snow you must leave this life and go. The poet writes his final line about things that could not be, the poet writes his final line for me."

They all clapped and all kissed Lilly and hugged her everyone was impressed but thought of it as just a poem and not a real event.

Soon after the discourse about the poetry they went to sleep, all but Tom who took the first watch, the first attack took place as a swarm of vampire bats flew over them followed by flying vampires. Lilly was suddenly lifted off the ground by one of the vampires; Tom took aim but was stopped by Fargo.

"Stop! You could hit Lilly," Fargo shouted.

"But they have taken her," Tom shouted back.

"They won't harm her, they want me," Siena said.

They continued to battle with the vampires until they disappeared and flew back to their master. The group were confused after Lilly had gone and they were determined to carry on and seek the Lost Poet in the fortress close by. Lilly had dropped her book when she was captured, so at least they could find the Lost Poet easily.

THE LOST POET

They noticed a fortress tower high upon a hill this is where the Lost Poet was said to dwell according to the poem. As they approached the tower they noticed a small door as they entered it they noticed stone steps that seemed to spiral to the top of the tower. They all went up the steps and arrived at another door, Tom pushed the door open and discovered a large room with a desk, a small table and a bed. On the table was a candle stick, a thick book and a coat hanging at the back of a chair. On the desk was another candlestick, an open book a quill and ink well. The bed had a cover over it with an interesting pattern on it; in the centre was an embroidered crest.

Suddenly to their astonishment a figure appeared near the desk, it was a man dressed in old medieval clothes, he had long white hair and looked about sixty. He looked directly at Siena and spoke to her in a gentle voice.

"Who do you seek?" he asked.

"I seek the lost poet," Siena replied.

"Why do you seek him?" he said suspiciously.

"He has something for me, I am on a quest to kill count Vermont," Siena said bravely.

"I am the Lost Poet, my name is John Gilbert Green and this is my home," Green said proudly.

"You live here in the tower?" Siena said looking around.

"Yes. This is my humble home and here is where I write my poems," Green pointed to his parchment on the desk.

"I just need a quill and I will be on my way, for we have a child to find, captured by the Count," Siena said sadly.

"I am sorry to hear that. I am but an image before you and my soul is also captured, I can only say follow your journey to your destination and you will find your child and me," Green said smiling.

With those words he vanished and the quill was in front of her to take to Count Vermont's castle. The Lost Poets voice could be still heard even after he had vanished, he was drawing the party to the castle in order to be found and set free. Siena led the partly out of the tower and back into the forest and towards another castle nearby where King Robert lived, he was a King without a kingdom.

A KING WITHOUT A KINGDOM

The man sat on the king's throne he seemed sad and lost wearing a hat and no crown, he was royal by blood but Count Vermont had invaded his kingdom with his vampires. The castle and the village was invaded and the people were either murdered with their bodies drained of blood, or had fled to the caves or other places of safety, some were turned into vampires and increased Count Vermont's ever growing army.

Siena and her friend walked towards the castle, small green man appeared holding a long spear. He had long black hair and a fat nose; he had a thick belt around his large waist and spoke with a high voice.

"Who goes there?" he said pointing his spear towards them.

"Its Siena and friends, we have come to see the King," Siena said positively.

"Siena, the vampire?" he asked.

"Yes that's me," Siena said. "But I am no longer known as a vampire."

"Siena I know all about you and Laura the witch," he said lowering his spear.

"You know Laura?" Siena asked.

"And I am Bramble and yes she is known throughout the kingdom," Bramble said smiling at Siena in a creepy kind of way.

Bramble led them to the King who remained sat on the throne, he sat stroking his beard as the party walked towards him and bowed.

"Tush, don't bow before me I am no King, see I have no kingdom," he swept his arms in each direction. "See no one but us."

"But you are still a King," Siena said.

"My kingdom was taken from me," the king stood up and shouted in temper. "I am not a King and my kingdom has been scattered into the wind, I have been left to care for myself and the Count lives in luxury with my servants and subjects. So come and laugh at the man who once was a King, I am now but a grain of sand on the beach or desert!" King Robert said bitterly.

"Then let us find Count Vermont and destroy his evil. Only then can we restore your throne and kingdom to what it was," Siena said.

"Yes your highness I am Tom the slayer and I have served you before as a blacksmith, Fargo was one of your guards so we have served you and will serve you again I promise," Tom said encouragingly.

"So how did you find me?" The king asked.

"Through an angel called Faith and a witch called Laura," Siena explained.

"I once condemned Laura as I did the vampires," King Robert said shyly.

"And yet you have statues of vampires all the way down the corridors of this castle?" Tom said confused.

"What are you talking about I have no statues of vampires!" King Robert said frowning.

At that moment the so called statues began to break away from the walls and flying towards the great hall, each detached themselves from the wall assisted by the wicked green goblin Bramble, who had obviously tricked and ambushed them. They all reached the hall and surrounded Siena and her friends.

"We have come for Siena, you must all surrender or die," one of the vampires said.

"Yes we want only Siena, kill the others," she hissed showing her fangs.

Bramble waved his spear about and tried to look menacing, but he just appeared silly in front of his vampire friends.

At that moment Laura appeared and immediately cast a spell on him leaving him in a giant bubble, he was kicking, yelling and trying to break free. As he was their mascot his capture confused the vampires for a moment. They looked at each other for inspiration and then attacked everyone in sight. Laura stunned each one with her wand while Tom and Siena destroyed them with their crossbows, firing deadly arrows into their hearts. Each one dispersed into dust and disappeared, the battle went on for half an hour until all the vampires were destroyed.

"Thank god that's over," Jack said sighing with relief.

"When are we going to be finally free from them vampires?" Tom said lowering his crossbow.

"When we destroy Count Vermont," Siena said sweeping back her hair.

"We should rest here tonight," Tom advised.

"Siena are you alright?" Jack asked.

"Yes apart from that strange little man," Siena looked at Bramble.

"He is of no importance," Tom said.

Bramble was removed from the bubble, bound with rope and led to the Counts castle; King Robert made peace with Laura and promised that when his kingdom was restored she would become his personal adviser.

Siena and her friends continued their quest, mindful of their mission to free the villagers and kill the enemy, removing the evil from the land. On their journey Fargo was attacked by blood sucking bats while on watch it was his biggest dread and he was saved by Siena and Tom who managed to fight them off. Later on their journey Siena had a snake wrapped around her neck which Fargo destroyed and threw it into a bush. Jacks fear were heights, walking over bridges made him nervous, looking down into rivers or rocky areas beneath him, they crossed many to reach the castle. As for Siena she was afraid of the full moon and although she wore the bracelets she was still affected by the desire for blood, she was looking forward to being human again.

"Siena I truly love you," Jack said sincerely.

"I love you too," Siena replied kissing Jack on the lips.

"But I fear myself and my desires," Siena looked down.

"I don't understand?" Jack replied.

"My thirst for blood, sometimes it is hard to fight and being near you makes it worse," Siena sighed and stood to her feet. "Will this nightmare ever end?"

"Be patient you are doing well," Jack advised her.

"Faith told me it would be difficult," Siena said looking into Jacks eyes.

"You will get there, reach your goal and we will be together," Jack explained holding her firmly by the arms.

Laura approached them with her long blonde hair flowing and her dress sparkling under the moonlight.

"It's a beautiful night," Laura said.

"Yes it is but the moon is full," Siena said pointing upwards.

"Be brave Siena and think of the future," Laura said smiling.

"I wanted Jack and I to live forever," Siena said.

"Who wants to live forever?" Laura said looking up at the moon.

"Not me," Jack said looking into Siena's eyes. "Definitely not me," Jack then looked across at the moon.

"I desire only one thing, a happy kingdom," Laura said touching them both on the arm. "And of course your happiness," Laura smiled and walked away.

THE EVIL COUNT VERMONT

After a long hazardous journey through a rough tureen with swamps, reptiles and other dangers, Siena and her friends reached Count Vermont's castle.

From the moment they arrived they could sense the danger and smell the rotting flesh of human and animal carcasses. Dried blood stains could be clearly seen on the filthy walls and floors, along with dust and cobwebs. The corridors were dimly lit and Tom advised them to use lighted wooden faggots as torches as they moved closer to the hall way.

Eventually they arrived in a large open area with an enormous stairway leading to the upper level with rooms running off in all directions. Suddenly the Count stood surrounded by his evil army of vampires, they were all assembled ready to attack, each eager to take the blood from the humans. Laura headed off to find Lilly and whoever else they had captured; she went straight towards the dungeons undetected making herself invisible. She used her wand to disarm the guard causing him to collapse in a heap on the floor. Then took the keys from his belt and unlocked the large door to the dungeon, finding many people inside including Lilly. However there was no sign of John Gilbert Green better known as the Lost Poet or his work, Lilly said that she had searched for him in the dungeons but to no avail.

The fighting was in progress when Laura returned; the vampires seemed to be everywhere until Laura cast a spell that drew them more together like a magnet. Count Vermont was fighting Siena, they were kicking and throwing objects at each other. Jack was trying to help but was knocked to the ground with the Counts mighty powerful force, he lay holding his head dazed by the blow to the head and winded by a kick to the stomach. Laura drew the other vampire's away in order to finally destroy them. Tom and Fargo were the main vampire slayers although other people joined in finding wooden stakes from broken chairs and other furniture. At last they were winning the battle as the last few vampires turned to dust and vanished. Siena was suddenly cornered by the Count he was about to kill Siena with her own stake when Tom shot an arrow into his heart, he dropped the stake and Siena picked it up. She made sure that she actually killed the Count by plunging the stake into him; she forced it in deeply then watched him disintegrate slowly. The vampire leader was finally dead, at that moment the Lost Poet returned he noticed Lilly first then the others. Fargo suddenly raced towards Siena in a rage brandishing a stake.

"There is one vampire left," Fargo shouted.

Tom reacted by shouting an arrow into Fargo's shoulder and Laura shielded Siena with her body. Laura fell to the ground she had been stabbed in the back and was bleeding, with all the confusion Bramble had escaped and headed for the woods. Laura passed away in the arms of Siena her last words were for King Robert.

"Siena help the king restore his kingdom and forgive Fargo because he fears you," She yelled in pain. "Burn my body and scatter my ashes beside a rock by the stream," with those words the witch died.

Jack explained to Fargo about Siena becoming human again at that moment Faith appeared.

"God is pleased with you Siena and you can remove the bracelets and return to the church with the items that you collected, for you are human again."

After fulfilling Laura's wishes and seeing the Kingdom restored Siena and Jack returned through the time portal and arrived at the church, they put all the items in the font and watched as a glowing light appeared and all the items vanished. Siena watched the sunlight shine through the windows of the church and for the first time for a long while was no longer afraid of the daylight for she was indeed human again.

CRACKED PORCELAIN

BROKEN WINGS AND LOST SOULS

A car races along a quiet road, being chased by a truck. It was travelling around hairpin bends and the two women in the car were frantically trying to shake off their pursuer. The truck hits the car once and almost causes the vehicle to leave the road; having failed the attempt the truck makes a second attempt to knock the car over the cliff. The car came to a halt and the driver of the truck revved the engine ready to ram the car and make a final attempt to knock the car over the cliff. The truck suddenly moved forward heading for the car everything seemed to go into slow motion.

One of the woman shouted, "Ruth put your bloody foot down!" she shouted.

"I cant it won't fucking work Cheryl," Ruth replied.

"We are going to die!" Cheryl shouted.

Suddenly the car moved forward and the truck raced forward over the cliff the driver was thrown clear as the truck hit rocks and exploded. After this took place Ruth explained that she had seen her former diseased girlfriend's ghost in the rear mirror and swore that she had saved their life. After she said this a man with an axe began smashing the car and trying to cut them to pieces. Moments later Ruth woke up and found blood on her legs and parts of her torso. Lying next to her was her girlfriend Cheryl fast asleep and unaware of Ruth's condition. After a while she too awoke and immediately noticed Ruth and the blood.

"Shit Ruth what's happened, have you been having nightmares again?" Cheryl said concerned.

Ruth nodded "Yes about Frank chasing us, but he survived the crash and came after us with an axe," Ruth said shaking.

Cheryl gave her a hug and kissed her on the cheek; she was aware of her nightmares and self-harming in her sleep. She knew how to deal with things although Ruth was the psychiatric nurse, Cheryl had learned a lot from her over the years that she had known her.

"You know that Franks dead don't you?" Cheryl said smiling.

"Yes of course," Ruth replied.

"We saw him die and so you're safe Ruth," Cheryl said.

"I know he died it's just me being silly," Ruth admitted.

Ruth got out of bed and headed for the bathroom, she stepped into the shower and washed away the blood from her body. She then washed her long dark hair and slim body; she then got out of the shower and put on her bathrobe. Cheryl had gone into the kitchen; she was making breakfast when Ruth appeared.

"How are you now?" Cheryl asked.

"Better thanks," Ruth replied, "Mm I love the smell of fresh toasted bread."

"Heaven to me dear," Cheryl replied.

"Kathy is picking me up for work," Ruth said.

"She is a good friend and colleague to you," Cheryl said.

Ruth had her breakfast and got ready to go to work; she kissed Cheryl and left the apartment. Kathy was waiting for Ruth in her car outside; she seemed worried as she sat gazing at the street ahead. Ruth rushed to the car and opened the door looking at her fair-haired friend and smiling cheerfully.

"Morning Kathy," Ruth said.

"Morning Ruth are you ok?" Kathy asked.

"Yes thanks are you?" Ruth replied.

"Yes I'm fine," Kathy said trying to hide her true feelings.

They arrived at work in time to get warm drinks before taking report from the night staff, a lot had happened to report and each patient was mentioned. The acute psychiatric ward was active with a variety of mental illnesses from bipolar to schizophrenia, all what Ruth termed as lost souls. People who have lost their way, people who need a sense of direction, ones who need help providing positively and not negative ideas. She had battled with Kathy to promote changes within the system of mental health, they had been friends for years and Kathy had supported Ruth through many problems.

After the ward round, the staff separated for a while concentrating on various aspects of the ward. Ruth and Kathy shared the drug round ensuring that each patient went to the serving hatch for their medication and then finding those who were in other areas. Observations were important and some patients were on special observations due to attempted suicide or misconduct. The corridors were busy with patients walking to or from their bedrooms; some were doing bizarre things, which was normal on an acute psychiatric unit. A patient called Alison was admitted because of postnatal depression, she would walk up and down the corridor quietly and sit in her room. Jessica had bipolar and was just going through her mania rushing down the corridor noisily and making fun of others. John was a schizophrenic who was having trouble managing his audible hallucinations using headphones in an attempt to drown them out with music.

Caroline who was suffering from clinical depression was having electric convulsive therapy (ECT), which Ruth attended and found it awful to watch, but it seemed to work as Caroline showed signs of improving. The need to shock someone in order to bring them back to reality seemed a little barbaric in today's society with all the drugs and various therapies, but as it still worked to a degree it remained an active treatment. Ruth never experienced it herself when she went through her depression, but her own history of mental illness stemmed from her child abuse or as she describes it, the dark and solitary place. She had been abused as a child and experienced mental and physical abuse from her former boyfriend Malcolm who was himself a psychopathic killer. He was responsible for the death of her girlfriend Pamela who was later discovered to be her sister.

They shared the same mother Sarah but Pamela died before her cousin Laura revealed the facts to Ruth.

Kathy was acting strange as she went about her duties on the ward as head nurse, it was unlike Kathy as she was so efficient and led the team successfully.

Ruth noticed that she was rather sharp at times and worked alone most of the day. Her whole behaviour was out of character for her, but she was reluctant to discuss what was wrong with her at this time. Ruth noticed her enter the kitchen and followed her hoping to get some answers from her and ease the tense atmosphere that was caused by her behaviour.

"Kathy what's wrong?" Ruth asked her.

"Nothing really," Kathy said abruptly.

"Come on you can't fool me, I fucking know you," Ruth said snapping back.

"I said nothing now leave it Ruth," Kathy insisted.

"But you have been acting odd today which is unlike you," Ruth said concerned.

"I am busy so let me get on," Kathy said leaving the kitchen.

Later that evening Kathy had dropped Ruth off at her apartment she had hardly spoken on the way home and merely said "Goodnight," and drove away. Ruth went straight into her apartment and was greeted by Cheryl.

"Hi Ruth how are you?" Cheryl said embracing her.

"I'm fine just a little tired," Ruth admitted.

At that moment the phone rang and Cheryl answered it.

"Just a moment," Cheryl said offering the phone to Ruth. "It's for you."

"It's probably Kathy she's been acting oddly today," Ruth said holding the phone to her head. "Hello," she said expecting to hear Kathy's voice.

"Hello," came a deep voice that startled Ruth.

"Do you know who this is, can you tell the voice?" the man continued in a deep voice.

"Who is this?" Ruth asked looking at Cheryl in bewilderment.

"Don't tell me you have forgotten me already?" He continued.

"It's Frank," He said in a menacing voice.

"No it can't be, is this some kind of sick fucking joke?" Ruth shouted.

"You wish bitch," Frank said laughing.

"Just stop bothering me you sick fucker," Ruth screamed down the phone.

That night Ruth had a nightmare about masks and skulls floating about. Ruth was dressed in a fashion costume with her girlfriend Pamela walking down a catwalk as they did in the fashion shows in the past. Pamela suddenly vanished and Ruth was left facing these masks alone, one mask came away from a face revealing her ex boyfriend Malcolm then another came away revealing his brother Frank. Ruth ran in slow motion trying to get away from them, but she eventually was captured and they attempted to pull her apart. She struggled free but fell backwards into the skulls; she tried to get up being pulled down into the skulls that were leaking blood. Eventually she got up but was stabbed by Frank and hit on the head with a baseball bat that Malcolm held firmly, he swung it once more and Ruth fell down.

Ruth awoke panicking and finding it hard to breath, she had hit her head on the cupboard door and Cheryl was attempting to calm her down.

"Ruth you're ok!" Cheryl shouted.

Ruth took deep breaths blowing air out and holding her chest as if her heart was going to explode. She became cold and clammy, the sweat pouring from her; gradually she calmed down and hugged Cheryl.

"What the fuck," Ruth said somewhat disorientated.

"Another nightmare Ruth?" Cheryl asked.

"Yes this time with Malcolm and Frank, when will it end?" Ruth said shaking.

"But Frank and Malcolm are dead," Cheryl said.

"I helped kill Malcolm with Pamela," Ruth said. "But Frank I spoke to him last night," Ruth said rocking on the bed.

"But we saw him die," Cheryl insisted.

"No we saw the truck go over the cliff that's all," Ruth replied.

"Yes and the truck exploded no one can survive that," Cheryl explained.

"I can believe anything from those crazy bastards," Ruth appeared very upset with tears in her eyes.

Ruth got out of bed and opened the curtains slightly; she looked across at the park entrance. "He's out there somewhere and he's after me," Ruth knew that he would pursue her it was just a matter of time before he would plan his next move.

Ruth was due to commence work the following day, she had not heard from Kathy, which was unusual as she often rang or called into her apartment, but today Kathy was on the late shift. Ruth had a busy day with a long ward round, Dr Geoffrey was in a chatty mood which meant that the round was even longer. Ward round on a mental health ward took place in a large room with all the disciplinary team present, this consisted of the psychiatric doctor, the registered mental health nurse (R.M.N), a occupational therapist and sometimes a community psychiatric nurse (C.P.N). The occasional patient was due for discharge and plans needed to be put in motion. The patient was going back into the community to live amongst people who probably wouldn't understand their illness and could treat them badly. A proper plan of action was required if the discharge was to be a success, this could involve a temporary stay in a small house with others in similar situations. They would have someone watching over them, observing their capabilities in managing finance, caring for themselves and being compliant with medication. The problem of relapse was so common in the community causing patients to return to the ward and requiring further treatment. Ruth had seen this many times, these are what they term as revolving doors, or Ruth's lost souls that required nurturing.

When Kathy arrived on shift Ruth was ready to hand over to her, the morning had proven fruitful and quite eventful judging by the general activity. The patients appeared restless and you feel the tension in the atmosphere as if something was going to blow.

"Ruth, are you alright?" Kathy asked.

"Yes I just keep getting nuisance phone calls," Ruth replied.,

"Really, don't let it bother you" Kathy said. "I get them too."

"From Frank?" Ruth said surprised.

"No, why that's impossible this guy must be an impostor?" Kathy said shaking her head.

"Maybe," Ruth replied confused.

"He is dead you saw him die remember?" Kathy said prompting her.

"Yes I saw the truck blow up so he fried," Ruth said pondering.

"Like a lobster," Kathy said laughing.

"It's really not funny," Ruth said frowning.

"Ok sorry, but he can't be alive can he?" Kathy said trying to reason with Ruth.

"I wish I could share your confidence," Ruth said adjusting her hair tying it in a pony tale with a brown bobble.

"Try not to think about it, you have been through enough lately," Kathy said stroking her arm.

Later that evening Ruth and Kathy went out for the evening joined by Cheryl, Sheena and Gloria. Ruth had invited them over to give them some good news; she was gleaming that night because all her friends were present. Her sisters Emma and Claire were present too; also keen to hear her news.

"Now that you are all here I wish to announce to you that Cheryl and myself are engaged and we are having a civil wedding."

Everybody cheered and applauded the surrounding tables also responded mostly positively by clapping. There were a few negative comments mainly by the homophobic people in the room; these were the ones to be ignored. One was heard to say 'How ridiculous whatever next.' Ruth never missed an opportunity to comment. "Ignorant bitch who the fuck does she think she is?" Ruth said aloud.

"Ignore her she's daft, hard up for a shag, try me or Ruth have some lesbian sex baby!" Cheryl shouted.

"Now girls concentrate on your wedding," Kathy advised.

"Oh yes my white dress, with frills, flowers and lace, I shall look such a fucking lady," Ruth said twirling around.

"What are you wearing Cheryl?" Gloria asked.

"I am wearing a blue dress with sparkling sequins and white laced cuffs," Cheryl added.

"I would like to get married," Sheena said looking at Gloria.

"Err, forget that babe I am straight," Gloria said laughing.

At that moment Angela walked in and immediately went over to Ruth and kissed her "Congratulations thank you for the phone call, I made it after all," Angela said.

Tara appeared at that moment "Do you need a photographer Ruth?"

Ruth stood up and ran towards her excitedly "Tara, how nice to see you."

"Angela told me about your wedding and I thought great Ruth is tying the knot at last," Tara said happily. "And I mean it I do insist on taking the photographs."

After hours of discussion about the wedding everybody parted company and went their separate ways, Ruth went back to the apartment with Cheryl, Emma and Claire. Claire wanted to speak to Ruth in private so they elected to make a drink for everyone, during the time they were in the kitchen Claire confided in Ruth.

"Ruth despite the fact that your real mother is Sarah, I still class you as my sister" Claire said

"Claire you are my sister, so what's the problem?" Ruth asked

"Well I am unsure about my sexuality, I don't know if I like men" Claire said bewildered.

"Who all have to find our own way" Ruth said

"But how do we know if it's the right way?" Claire said worried

"You will know it takes time to know for sure, but the feelings inside tell you where you need to be" Ruth explained "Just don't think a bad experience as a child makes you gay" Ruth explained "Child abuse is a bad thing and it is easy to blame every man for one bad bastard, but date others and experience heterosexual relationships first then you will know".

"Thanks Ruth you're the best" Claire said hugging her.

"Your welcome sister" Ruth said smiling.

"Ruth, are you working tomorrow?" Claire asked

"No why?" Ruth said inquisitively

"Lets go on a shopping spree" Claire said excitedly

"Sure that sounds nice" Ruth said with a finger on her lips "Shhh don't lCheryl to think I am spending our wedding money.

The next day Ruth and Claire left for the city, Cheryl had left early to go away on a art trip preparing for an exhibition called 'Life in a jar' based on a book by Stephen Sutton the idea was to take an ambiguous title and draw, paint or create anything around the title. Cheryl chose a jar with a human model inside symbolising restriction or limitations, over a hundred artist contributed to this exhibition. This made

Cheryl feel good and that she had something to offer the world, it also gave Cheryl a sense of worth and achievement.

Meanwhile Ruth was enjoying her shopping spree looking around many shops and buying clothes, shoes and hats. Ruth and Claire were very close and enjoyed every moment of time together, shopping, eating out and drinking together. Then Claire led Ruth into a tattoo shop so that Claire could have a tattoo of a butterfly on her foot. Ruth sat looking around the studio at the many designs, and then she noticed an angel, which reminded her of Pamela.

"I would love to have that on my shoulder" she said "It would be a memory of Pamela".

"So have it" Claire said encouragingly

"No I shouldn't" Ruth replied

"Why not it's a good idea" Claire said

"Ok I will" Ruth agreed, "Does it hurt?"

"Honestly Ruth you have been through so much and your worried about a little discomfort". Claire laughed

On their way around the shops they met Laura, so Ruth told her the news about her wedding but Laura wasn't sure how to take the news. Laura wasn't quite sure what she thought about Ruth's relationship with Cheryl, she was never sure about the lesbian thing as she called it. She loved Ruth but not her lifestyle, but Ruth's idea was to love people for who they are. She believes its all about people being genuine and truthful to themselves, people respect honest people and who can do exactly what they want to do as long as it doesn't physically harm others.

Claire stayed with Ruth that night they drank wine and spoke until two am then they slept until late morning. They went for breakfast in a nearby café on the way they met one of the neighbours called Paul a slim and well-spoken man who specialised in law. He sat staring at Ruth on another table, he hardly moved for at least half an hour; Ruth felt a little uneasy and soon left the café.

A week passed and she met Paul going into the same café, Paul seemed embarrassed at seeing her and spoke to her.

"Ruth I wanted to see you" Paul explained

"So now you've seen me" Ruth said suspiciously

"Ruth don't be like that" Paul said feeling hurt

"Well what do you expect, the last time I was in here you just stared at me" Ruth said looking at him and pointing her finger "How did you expect me to react, I find that creepy" Ruth was determined to get her point over.

"I'm sorry but to be honest I really like you" Paul explained

"Oh so its love or lust then" Ruth said bluntly

"No not at all I think you're beautiful and in my opinion it's a waste, you being a lesbian" Paul said sincerely

"Well to you it must be you being a full blooded heterosexual male" Ruth began to feel relaxed in his company.

"I guess that I will have to continue dreaming. Paul said jokingly

"Well to be honest you do make me laugh" Ruth admitted

"As long as I amuse you" Paul said smiling

"I suppose if I were honest if I was heterosexual you would be the man for me" Ruth said smiling back.

"Really, then I feel better for that" Paul said

"I am pleased about that Paul honestly" Ruth said with sincerity.

They left the café, hugged and kissed and then parted Cheryl had just got back from her trip and saw them kissing.

Ruth returned to her apartment surprised at seeing Cheryl, she noticed the expression on her face and the cold reception that she received.

"Cheryl what's wrong" Ruth asked

"I notice you have a tattoo" Cheryl said

"Yes an Angel" Ruth said "Do you like it?"

"I suppose that is Pamela?" Cheryl said sharply

"She was my sister you know" Ruth said angrily

"And your lover" Cheryl said

"Oh I see you're jealous of a dead person" Ruth said

"What are you up to I saw you kissing Paul outside the café, do you know what you want or which way you want to go?" Cheryl said

"For fuck sake Cheryl he is a friend I don't like him that way and as for Pamela "I explained about her being my sister and now I think of her as my sister ok" Ruth said pacing up and down.

"I suppose so" Cheryl said sitting on the settee

"If you don't trust me what is the use marrying me, I am honest and true to you but you don't trust me".

"I am sorry but maybe I am insecure" Cheryl admitted

"Well don't be so fucking stupid and grow up" Ruth said walking towards the bathroom.

Cheryl left Ruth to calm down before knocking on the bathroom door, she had been crying and felt guilty making accusations about Ruth.

"Ruth please come out" Cheryl pleaded

There was a silence Cheryl was worried that Ruth had done something stupid so she knocked on the door again.

"Ruth!" she shouted

The door was unlocked and Ruth appeared looking tired and upset, she looked at Cheryl who looked sheepish at her, with her eyes pleading forgiveness.

"I am really sorry Ruth I have been so foolish" Cheryl said

"Its ok lets get a drink" Ruth said

"So is the wedding still on?" Cheryl asked

"Of course" Ruth replied walking forward with her arms out to hug Cheryl.

They had supper then went to bed and continued their conversation cuddled up together in bed.

"Ruth I know you have been through more than anyone else I know and endured as much as anyone can, but try to let me in, please". Cheryl said

"I will try to do so honestly" Ruth said "But sometimes my head is fucked and the ghosts from my past haunt me, I am like a bird with broken wings". Ruth explained. "So how do I help my lost souls?"

"Let me mend your wings so that you can deal with your lost souls" Cheryl offered.

"Ok heal me and let me learn to love you deeply" Ruth said kissing Cheryl on the lips and caressing her body.

"Let me release the demons from your head and the badness that lurks within" Cheryl said kissing her back.

The next morning Ruth returned to work happily knowing that her future was planned and she had more to look forward to as she had a wedding on the horizon. She picked Kathy up from her house and headed to the hospital and the acute mental health ward that they had worked on for so many years together.

"Good morning Kathy" Ruth said

"Morning Ruth" Kathy replied

Kathy seemed distant again and was just nodding, as Ruth spoke none stop about her wedding all the way to the hospital. When they arrived Ruth spoke to Kathy in the staff room with others present.

"You know that I am getting married" Ruth began

"Think so Ruth you have told me every detail to date" Kathy said

"Well we want you to be maid of honour" Ruth said

"Don't you mean maid of dishonour" Kathy replied

"I said that last night" Ruth said laughing

"Cheeky bitch" Kathy replied

"Well will you?" Ruth asked

"Depends whether I am here or not" Kathy said

"Fuck off Kathy of course you will be" Ruth seemed puzzled by what Kathy had said.

Suddenly one of the staff commented

"A wedding for gays, how silly, a civil wedding they call it, I call it gays showing off, flaunting their sexuality". The woman said scornfully

"Well I'm not going" she continued.

"Who invited you?" Ruth asked

The woman bowed her head in shame as she didn't realise that she was speaking so loud and was overheard by Ruth. Kathy looked at Ruth as if she had spoken out of turn, but Ruth continued to speak to the woman.

"Well Kathy some people consider that their life is the only way to live, the pompous arrogant fuckers. Yes I mean you Janet oh look Anna is back as Janet thinking she is perfect, the one who destroyed Pamela and now wants to destroy my relationship with Cheryl too". Ruth said angrily.

"Ruth not now please" Kathy said embarrassed

"It has to be said Kathy" Ruth continued "Bad mouthed bitch"

"Ruth!" Kathy shouted slamming her fist on the table.

Ruth looked at Kathy in shock "My god you're defending her against me"

"For Christ sake Ruth its not all about you, stop being selfish" Kathy looked angry and pale.

Ruth looked at Kathy in disbelief she tried to touch her on the arm but Kathy shrugged her off "Don't please" Kathy said coldly looking away from Ruth.

Ruth looked at the staff who were in the room, including Janet and then walked out of the staff room slamming the door on her way out.

Later Kathy approached Ruth to apologise, Ruth was still upset not by being shouted at she was used to that, but by Kathy not defending her as she had done many times before.

"I am truly sorry Ruth" Kathy said

"Its fine" Ruth said

"No it bloody well isn't fine" Kathy continued, "I am not fine"

"What do you mean" Ruth said looking at Kathy

"I have a lump on my breast" Kathy said pointing to her left breast

"Shit no" Ruth said shocked

"I have known about it for months but couldn't tell you" Kathy said

"Why I am your friend" Ruth said with tears in her eyes

"That's exactly why, because I am tough, strong and dependable, well taking a look at the tough woman now" Kathy said with tears trickling down her face.

"Oh my god Kathy not you" Ruth hugged her and they both wept together,

"Now you have to be the tough one Ruth, the cancer has already spread and I will have to have treatment soon". Kathy explained.

"I am not hearing this, god I feel sick" Ruth said trying to keep strong.

"Come on Ruth I need your strength right now" Kathy held Ruth tightly

"Yes your right I must be strong for you" Ruth tried to control her emotions.

Ruth's mind was distracted by the activity on the ward Trevor who was by polar was going through his manic period dashing up and down the ward shouting. While Sally was repeating herself constantly saying 'it's me oh yes it's me'. Ruth and Kathy shared the drug round that morning, watching each patient take their medication correctly and not storing them in their mouth. Kimberly was prepared for her electric convulsive therapy (ECT) to jolt her back to reality.

Ruth tried to be a tower of strength for Kathy and avoided telling her of the repeated phone calls from Frank. She took Kathy to some of her chemo sessions and returned her home to her family but underneath she felt as if she was losing another mother figure that she adored even more than her stepmother Diane. Her rock and protector was ill and fading before her eyes and she couldn't stop this from happening. Ruth looked back on the many times that Kathy had helped her over the years. She had defended her when she went off with a patient called Pamela to do modelling and helped her back to nursing. She was there when Raven the schizophrenic tried to kill her and through much more. The clock was now ticking for her and Ruth felt helpless, unable to stop this deadly disease from killing her friend.

Ruth walked through the park with her mind drifting back to past events such as when they went out drinking, times at work with problem patients. But what was more important Kathy was instrument in helping her to recover from depression and become re-established on the ward as a qualified psychiatric nurse. Ruth remembered the special loving relationship they had with each other as friends, hugging each other in appreciation for what they did for each other. Ruth thought back to the battle between Raven and herself and how Kathy fought with her until the death of Raven who was killed when a branch landed upon her penetrating her body. Ruth stood by the tree where Raven died and visualised her last moments of life in this place in the park.

Ruth also was aware that Malcolm her ex psychopathic boyfriend murdered someone near here with a baseball bat. She thought about the disasters that occurred, due to Malcolm and his brother Frank in their attempt to kill Ruth. She thought of her brother and sisters and the dreadful childhood being abused and her dark lonely place in the wardrobe, where she hid many times from her abuser. Kathy had even helped her to cope with this in a way that no one else could. She showed Ruth how to think ahead and not dwell on past events, to act positively with a goal in mind. As she continued walking she passed an old man in a wheelchair they were heading towards the apartment building where Ruth lived. The man spoke to the girl but Ruth was too far away to here as she headed out of the park gates.

"That's Ruth" the man said

"You mean the one who killed your brother?" The woman asked

"Yes Malcolm and her apartment is this way" He pointed to the apartment ahead.

Ruth walked to Diane's house, she was apprehensive about entering the house due to so many bad memories there. As she entered the house things came flooding back, such as the death of her so called father, the rows with her step mother Diane and Sister Emma, not to mention her abuse as a child.

Emma and Claire sat in the living room as Ruth entered, both greeted her with open arms, Emma's baby Lucy was in a carry cot by the settee.

"Aw how is Lucy?" Ruth asked

"She's fine" Emma replied

"So who's making a drink then?" Ruth asked cheekily

"I will I suppose" Emma said reluctantly

"I must use your toilet" Ruth said heading towards the stairs

She walked up the stairs and entered the toilet; after she had been she walked into the bedroom that she had as a child. Here was where all the abuse took place years ago, but it was like yesterday. The wardrobe that she used to hide in which she called her solitude of safety was still there old and tatty but the even the loose handle was never fixed. Ruth reflected back to the dreadful incidents that scarred her life forever, she became anxious and started to tremble. Her heart was pounding and tears trickled down her cheeks, she could smell aftershave and sweat mixed together which to her was a ghastly odour that made her rush to the toilet and vomit. The fact that she could visualise in her mind all the horrific scenes from her abuse made her stomach churn and caused her such pain.

At that moment Claire appeared and comforted her, she too had been abused in this house and in the same room.

"Are you alright Ruth?" she asked

"Yes just the past rearing its ugly head like an unwanted growth" Ruth replied.

"I know what you mean" Claire said concerned

"It fucks my head right up" Ruth continued.

"Me too" Claire said looking back into the room.

"They ought to knock this place down, either that or burn it down" Ruth said angrily.

"We should move somewhere else, too many bad memories" Claire said

"Emma won't move you know that, she was never affected by abuse" Ruth said bitterly.

"Then lets talk to her and explain how we feel, I am sure David will agree". Claire insisted.

They went downstairs and began to discuss it with Emma

"No way, I am not leaving this house no matter what happens" Emma insisted

"But just think of all the bad memories Emma" Claire said trying to reason with her.

"For fuck sake Emma see reason" Ruth said annoyed

"This is your idea Ruth and you don't even live here" Emma snapped back at Ruth.

"Yes but I do" Claire said.

"So why don't you live with Ruth" Emma said holding the baby "Lucy is going to grow up here".

"This fucking place should be burnt down" Ruth shouted

"And me in it I suppose for wanting to be here" Emma said becoming tearful.

"Don't be like that I only want what's best for us all as a family" Ruth said

"Family is that what you call us, Mother died because of you" Emma said then realised what she had said in anger. "Sorry I didn't mean that".

"No but you said it" Claire said defending Ruth

"I have to go I will catch you later, Kath needs me" Ruth said walking towards the front door.

"How is she?" Claire asked

"Very ill she's having chemotherapy, she's sick, tired and fed up". Ruth said opening the front door.

"If we can help let us know" Emma said concerned

"You have enough to do" Ruth replied walking outside.

Later that day Ruth was sitting next to Kathy's hospital bed with Gloria and Sheena, they were discussing wedding plans.

"So Ruth, who have you got to making your cake?" Sheena asked

"Don't know yet" Ruth replied

"We can organise that" Gloria said

"Really?" Ruth said surprised

"Yes a special treat" Sheena said

"With roses and colourful like your life" Gloria said laughing

"That's true" Sheena agreed.

"Cheeky lot anyone would think I am someone who lives the high life when I'm on an emotional roller coaster half the time with a fucked head" Ruth said.

"Language" Kathy said waking up.

"Sorry Kathy" Ruth said looking at the others.

Later that day Ruth was about to drive past Diane's house heading home when the road was blocked ahead. She noticed fire engines and an ambulance; suddenly she panicked and ran towards a crowd of people, Diane's house was on fire. Flames engulfed the living room and the firemen were busy trying to put it out, Ruth tried to fight through the crowd panicking. Suddenly she saw Claire and David, standing with blankets around them talking to police men.

"Where is Emma and Lucy?" Ruth shouted

"Still inside, they are upstairs" Claire said in tears.

"My god no" Ruth said putting both hands to her mouth.

Suddenly two firemen came rushing out just in time for the fire to spread upstairs; one was carrying a baby and the other supporting Emma.

At that point a police officer approached Ruth, he appeared very stern.

"Are you Ruth?" One of the officers said

"Yes I am" Ruth replied

"Then I need you to come with me to the station" He continued

"Why what's wrong?" Ruth asked

"Someone answering your description was seen in the vicinity and one witness said that you started the fire" He said

"She didn't do it" Claire said in her defence.

The officers led Ruth past the ambulance where Emma was just entering in a wheelchair. Emma looked at Ruth and shouted coughing at the same time.

"Well you got your wish, the house is burnt down" Emma said then looked away.

Ruth remained silent and entered the police car, Claire joined Ruth while David went with Emma.

Ruth and Claire seemed to be in the interview room for a long time before two officers appeared doing their usual routine of good cop, bad cop questioning Ruth about the arson.

"Come on Ruth you were heard to have said 'I would love to put a torch to this fucking house and burn it down' those are your words aren't they?" The bad cop asked.

"You are very attractive a model on Television" the good cop said smiling.

"Did you say that?" the bad cop repeated.

"Yes I did but I didn't do it" Ruth insisted

"But you had a bad time in that house, nobody blames you for doing it" Good cop said.

"So just admit it" Bad cop said

"Someone was seen there like me and I was at the hospital visiting a friend" Ruth explained.

"An alibi but you could have arranged for someone else to do it" Bad cop continued.

"For fuck sake you are really annoying me, I said that I was with a sick friend and besides I would never cause a fire or my family harm".

The interview continued for half an hour and then Ruth was released from the police station and they both went to Ruth's apartment.

That evening Ruth's phone rang it was Frank, Ruth put the phone on speaker for all present to hear.

"Ruth how did you like the fire, this is just the start I am going to make you suffer for the death of Malcolm". Frank said in a wicked voice.

"You're a tucking maniac" Ruth shouted.

"I sent Raven to kill you, she failed so I sent others and will keep on sending them until your dead". Frank continued making threats towards Ruth.

"Stop all this madness you sick bastard". Ruth said hysterically.

"Am I getting to you Ruth?" Frank said sneering.

"You think your so fucking clever, but your just a sick shit" Ruth shouted even louder.

Everything went silent then the call ended, Ruth raced into the bathroom to be sick. Emma was present to hear Frank along with David, Claire and Cheryl, all witnessed that Frank was behind the arson.

The police were informed about the phone call and they began investigations into Frank's whereabouts. At least Ruth was no longer a suspect and could continue helping Kathy, nursing her through her last days.

Kathy was transferred to an hospice and Ruth arranged time off work to care for her there, she insisted on washing her and making her look nice. She was in and out of consciousness during the day and night, but Ruth never left her side.

Ruth knew her death was immanent, it was just a matter of days or hours who knew as some people say it was in the hands of god.

But one sunny morning Ruth was looking out of the window at the swaying trees and the cherry blossom, when a bird fell to the ground with its wing broken. Ruth was unable to reach it as it struggled to get up, it was helpless and defenceless like so many people she had seen before including herself. At that moment Kathy opened her eyes and tried to focus on Ruth, she smiled and tried to speak despite all the morphine that she was receiving through a syringe driver.

"Ruth you are in my dreams, I am pleased you are with me" Kathy said in a slurred manner.

"I am with you Kathy, I will never leave you" Ruth said gripping her hand

"Bless you for taking care of broken wings and lost souls" Kathy continued

"You are the same Kathy, you mend wings and care for lost souls" Ruth said trying to hold back her tears.

"God I am scared Ruth, I am afraid to die" Kathy admitted.

"Please don't be let yourself sleep in peace" Ruth felt tears trickling down her face as she notices Kathy passing away.

Kathy took her last breath and Ruth put her head on her chest and wept. At this moment Sheena and Gloria appeared and tried to consol her.

"No not Kathy, my rock, my dear friend she can't die I need her" Ruth shouted

Sheena and Gloria cried too as the nurses rushed forward to assist, Ruth refused to let go of Kathy clinging hold of her dead body. Eventually Sheena and Gloria managed to free her from Kathy and escort her to a quiet room.

"Why didn't god take me, I did ask him, I did" Ruth said even though she doubted gods existence.

Gloria just held Ruth tightly in her arms, while Sheena held Ruth's hand they sat for a moment while the nurses took care of Kathy behind some screens.

"I saw a bird with a broken wing, it was outside the window" Ruth said pointing to the window.

"Someone put it in a box" Sheena said "They took it away".

Kathy's funeral took place at the same crematorium as Diane's and Pamela's funeral, many people attended as she was loved by many people. Ruth reflected back to Diane's funeral and remembered Laura telling her about her real mother Sarah, if only she had known her and shared her love. Varied arrangements of flowers were present, displayed outside with the names of friends and relatives who rarely saw Kathy. Kathy was a private person as the vicar pointed out, she chose her friends carefully but loved Ruth like a daughter and often protected her.

Ruth returned to work she sat with Kimberly who was discussing her depression and how the E.C.T had benefited her, she was about to go home and seemed happy. Trevor dashed past them going through another manic moment, he was shouting expressing strange thoughts. Alison a rather large lady who suffering from schizophrenia sat staring into space with headphones on, evidently blocking out the voices in her head. These people were Ruth's lost souls and she loved them, she in fact would be lost without them and she often imagined Kathy was with her to share them and their needs. Kimberly looked at Ruth for the first time since her admission, she used to just put her head down and look at the floor. She had beautiful blue eyes that were once dull, now they seemed to sparkle like diamonds in a ring.

"Thank you for helping me" Kimberly said touching Ruth's hand

"Your we come, I hope all goes well for you" Ruth said smiling.

"I was sorry to hear about Kathy" Kimberly said looking at Ruth's large brown eyes "You are so attractive like a model".

"Yes well let's not go there" Ruth said laughing.

"Ok I won't peruse that" Kimberly laughed for the first time since admission.

Trevor raced around them laughing in a more mocking way, then coming out with a random comment. While Alison removed her headphones and walked out of the room.

It was a week later when Frank began to call Ruth again, he became more intense with his calls and sent one of his friends to damage Ruth's car. It was the woman who resembled Ruth who burnt down Diane's house, unfortunately for her the police were watching the car at the time. They anticipated another attack on Ruth or her family and sat in a car near to Ruth's apartment, seeing the woman starting to smash the windows with a metal bar rushed over and arrested her. They took her to the police station and questioned her, after a while she confessed and with little persuasion she told the police where Frank lived.

The police raided Frank's home discovering photos of Ruth and her family displayed on a wall, with details of addresses of family and friends. He had planned out events and even named who was allocated to harm or kill each person, but the final plot was for him to shoot Ruth with his own gun near the park. What was more worrying it was planned for that day, even the time was displayed for 21.00 and it was now 20.40. One of the officers reached for his radio and alerted the police control centre.

Frank was waiting for Ruth to appear, he was sat in his electric wheelchair hidden under a tree. He was hiding in the shadows and called Ruth as she was passing close by, holding his gun out aiming it at Ruth's head.

"Ruth" He shouted

Ruth looked at him and froze on the spot, she was completely motionless as she noticed his finger on the trigger. Her whole life passed before her as she waited for him to squeeze the trigger and shoot her dead.

"I have waited a long time for this Ruth, now at last I can kill you" Frank said in a menacing voice.

"Go ahead kill me after all you have ruined my life" Ruth said with her arms out

"I just want to see you suffer a moment longer, plead for your worthless life" Frank gloated "I want to see the fear on your face and" Frank was interrupted by Ruth

"Fuck you, your just a sad pathetic bastard like your brother Malcolm, go ahead shoot me" Ruth shouted in rage, but quivering inside.

"That's it now you die" Frank said pulling the trigger

A loud bang echoed down the street and Ruth fell backwards with the impact of the bullet, Franks wheelchair then raced forward and his eyes widened as he saw a bus heading at great speed before him, the impact knocked the chair across the road and he catapulted out into the road. He was hit by another heavy vehicle and was crushed under a wheel, his stomach burst open and his intestines spread across the road. When examined the police noticed that his head had been decapitated at some point. Blood was everywhere and even present in the wheelchair indicating that he must have been injured when the bus hit him.

Ruth lay on the ground Cheryl and Claire raced over the road to reach her, the police were already there examining her.

"Is she dead?" Claire asked.

Ruth opened her eyes and looked up at the crowd of faces everything was blurry, but she did see Pamela in the background.

"No she was lucky just a shoulder wound" one of the policemen said

"Ouch it fucking hurts" Ruth said touching the blood on her clothing

"She's ok she's cursing and swearing as usual" Cheryl said smiling.

"Are you her family?" An ambulance driver asked

"Yes we are" Claire said smiling at Cheryl

"You go to the hospital with her Claire" Cheryl insisted.

In the ambulance Ruth continued complaining on the journey to the hospital

"Fuck it hurts cant you give me anything for pain" Ruth said rolling her eyes

"Ruth please they are doing their best your lucky to be alive" Claire explained

"Oh am I, is that so you try getting shot" Ruth continued

"At least you're alive" Claire said annoyed

"What makes you think I want to be" Ruth shouted

"You selfish bitch" Claire said slapping her across the face.

"Claire" Ruth said holding her face

"Well sorry but we all love you" Claire said feeling guilty.

Ruth became silent and looked at Claire holding her hand.

"I love you Claire" Ruth said smiling

"Piss off Ruth" Claire said smiling back

Emma was at the hospital greeting them in, David hovered in the background pacing up and down. Once the bullet had been removed from her shoulder Ruth was taken to the ward to recover. She was surrounded by admirers and each one was discussing the civil wedding, they spoke about dresses and cakes.

Emma sat with Ruth alone at one point discussing family and where they had been given a home.

"Ruth you were right, there were too many bad memories there especially for you and Claire, so we have a new home and its really nice" Emma explained.

"I am pleased for you Emma" Ruth said smiling

"So what happened with Frank" Emma asked.

"I don't really know Emma, things happened so fast" Ruth sighed "He held the gun up shot at me, but I swear that I felt someone push me hard on the shoulder and I fell to the ground. My other shoulder was burning and I felt a sharp pain then passed out". Ruth explained.

"You were pushed?" Emma asked

"Yes definitely pushed, then I came round and began hallucinating seeing Pamela". Ruth said bewildered

"Christ Ruth you did see her she saved your life, she is your guardian angel" Emma insisted.

"No way" Ruth dismissed her

"It the only explanation and apparently Frank's electric chair went out of control into the road" Emma explained

"So what happened to him?" Ruth asked

"Don't worry the twat is dead, his body was torn apart by two vehicles" Emma went on.

"Nice way to go for a psycho" Ruth said bitterly.

Emma hugged Ruth and kissed her gently on the cheek

"Well sister lets home all your problems are over" Emma said sincerely

"Look ahead and continue dealing with my lost souls at work and look forward to the wedding with my friends and family".

The civil wedding took place as arranged many people attended and shared the happy day with Ruth and Cheryl, it was published in all the gay magazines and even mentioned on the local news. Ruth returned to the ward feeling Kathy's presence as she went about her routine, taking care of her broken wings and lost souls.

ALL ABOUT FAITH - UNDERSTANDING JODIE

Faith is a guardian angel that had to learn about people, she lived on earth for a short time observing humans and asking her superiors a lot of questions so that she could fully understand them and how to deal with them in a caring manner. But Faith had made mistakes and needed to rectify this by helping humans to adjust their life and turn to god. She knew the consequences of failing to protect people and to be cast out of heaven would be so humiliating for her.

One of her earliest experiences of human behaviour was way back in history during the life of Jesus Christ. After witnessing his horrific treatment and death by the Romans she became very sad and reluctant to help human beings.

But her superiors had other ideas as they attempted to make her see that humans are good people in general. She had been sent to earth in order to study humans and appreciate that they were imperfect, She helped human's in the past but being on the earth made her realise that they were sensitive, loving people who were influenced by good and evil, confused by which path to follow. The angels had free will and some left heaven being cast out by God, these were known as the fallen angels who caused havoc on earth since their departure from heaven. They were classed as demons and their only aim on earth was to destroy anything that is good, Faith and other angels who were loyal to god attempted to defend humans. God was pleased with Faith and Harmony along with the other angels who helped to save the earth from destruction, But Faith once struggled to help people and needed to prove that she was a good faithful servant of god. She had defeated Dawn a fallen angel and her sister Sonia in the past, now she had a new adversary called Fiona who was sent to collect as many souls as possible. Fiona was stronger in mind and body than Sonia who questioned her master's motives and right to challenge God. She searched the deepest crevices of the earth for the most evil people that she could find, this included prisons and asylums hoping to convert everyone to the art of evil.

One such target was Jodie Brown a school girl who grew to hate people and the system not knowing who to trust or like, her life spiralled into a pit of darkness and she eventually was sent to prison. It was at this point that Faith appeared in her Cell like a strong light Faith was dressed in a white glowing dress and holding a key in her left hand. She had long fair hair and a radiant smile, her presence frightened Jodie.

"Who are you?" Jodie asked

"I am Faith, I am an angel who has come to you with a message of hope" Faith explained.

"Are you fucking kidding me?" Jodie asked abruptly.

"Trust me I am here to help you" Faith continued

"Help me I am beyond help and now I am even hallucinating, prison food must be bad". Jodie said laughing.

"How can I convince you that I am real?" Faith said

Jodie moved forward and touched her at this point a prison warden looked in the hatch on the door, he saw Faith in the cell.

"Who are you and how did you get in there with Jodie?" He asked

At that moment she disappeared and reappeared after he closed the hatch

"You see I was seen by him too" Faith said

"My god you're a real angel" Jodie said

"Yes now you believe me, so do you want to turn your life around?" Faith asked

At this point another angel appeared, she was black with gorgeous brown eyes.

"This is Harmony my friend she can also help you" Faith said pointing to Harmony

"Hi Jodie" Harmony said politely.

"So tell us how this all began" Faith said sitting on the floor with Harmony.

"It all began at school I was being bullied for being dyslexic and gay, not a good combination I know, but that's me" Jodie admitted.

"That's your story?" Harmony asked

"No let me tell you the rest of my crap life so far" Jodie insisted.

REFLECTING BACK

It was just another winter's morning, as a blanket of snow lay thick on the ground. I suppose that I would be regarded as a typical thirteen-year-old girl wearing my school uniform with pride and carrying my school bag on my back. I suppose you would consider me pretty with my tanned skin, perfect teeth and large hazel eyes. I am slim and conscious of my weight never eating at regular times with a highly active lifestyle that burns my metabolism like a girl on fire. I always put my hair into a pony tail, I suppose the colour is alright two tone brown, but no doubt when I am older I could be a blonde like my mother.

My parents, well what can I say we live in a nice house, both my parents work so we look after ourselves most of the time. My younger brother Gary needs watching though, he is so naughty at times. My older brother Tom who is sixteen takes care of us both and walks Gary to school. I am old enough to make my own way to school, although the bullies are always there to ruin my day. I wonder what it will be today stealing my clothes from the changing room, flicking a towel at my Derry air or ruining my artwork. Maybe their simple minds will conjure up a new way of making my life a misery.

On my way to school I enjoy walking down the avenue, I walk through an avenue of trees and gaze up at the long thin branches imagining I am in some enchanted Forrest in a fantasy world. I can admire the snow on the trees and feel the breeze blowing gently on my face. It is blowing a spray of snow down like flower being sieved onto a table; I wish I had my paints right now so that I could paint this picture. Art is my favourite subject I spend so much time in that classroom, I feel that I can escape from life in my pictures. I can create my own fantasy and dictate who does what and be a heroine with admirers all around me.

As I left the avenue I continued to walk to school my dreams were suddenly shattered by the impact of a snowball to my head, then another to my back. The school bullies throwing snowballs at me one after the other surrounded me. I let out a scream that must have sounded worse than any horror movie; it was that loud penetrating the school building, it was almost blood curdling. O.K not that bad but enough to fetch the teachers out and stop the bullies in their tracks.

"Right Johnson, Dawson and Julie inside now" came the booming voice of Mr Gilbert the maths teacher.

He was enough to scare anyone with his tall and broad physique, he was an ex boxer and one teacher that you would never answer back. He watches each of them go inside and gave them a look of disgust for being bullies.

Then he looked at me a girl that was wet and shivering with cold, suddenly his facial expression changed from annoyance to sympathy as he spoke to me in a gentle voice

"You had better go inside and get dry, Mrs Cooper will help you"

This was like music to my ears the teacher that I drooled over was going to dry my hair and help me to change. My god could life get any better I had the worlds most beautiful woman as my teacher. Mrs Cooper led me into a room in the gym and began drying my hair as luck would have it she was wearing a white blouse that had a few buttons open. I could clearly see part of her breasts wobbling as she was vigorously rubbing at my hair. I was in ecstasy the whole time until she turned me round to dry the back; even then her knees were rubbing against my buttocks. The whole experience was very brief but enough to affect me physically.

I rejoined the class and sat through geography, but instead of studying the contours of land I was back with Mrs Cooper studying the contours of her body. This clearly questioned my sexuality, if I fancied the female teacher like this then was I a raving lesbian or maybe I was bi sexual?. I never thought of it before I was evidently growing up and noticing the human form. Sex classes were no help discussing reproduction and nothing to do with gender types, comparing masculinity and femininity as a way of spotting the difference between male and female.

The best part of geography was the school bell for the end of period; I have never seen a class empty as quickly as Miss Hammonds. She had to be the world's most boring person she could cause the entire class to go to sleep in seconds with her droning voice and she doesn't stop for breath. I have actually seen her turn blue before she began to breath normally, what's more if she did collapse with her weight she could crush you instantly into mush.

I entered the toilets and as usual the female bullies were stood talking about boys and who would get a date first. I entered one of the cubicles and was suddenly drowned with water from the girls using plastic cups one after another. I how I wished that they would find something original to do, the predictability of water being thrown over me I should carry an umbrella with me everywhere I go.

Again I was thinking about that blonde twenty five year old teacher Mrs Cooper, I am going to date her definitely and she will take me back to her place and show me a good time. We would have Milkshake and chicken burgers with extra mayonnaise licking it off with her tongue. At that moment my fantasy ended with the banging of the door and a loud voice.

"Jodie Brown hurry up your late for English" the voice said

English a lesson that I attend but never like, it's so hard to understand and I always end up daydreaming. I can't concentrate and get into so much trouble with the teachers. I spend most of my school life in front of the headmaster listening to his lectures on if he lived his life again he would be a brain surgeon or dentist, honestly I would sooner be punished by having the Cain by Mrs boring Hammond. God bless the old dears bloomers I bet she hasn't had a man since the turn of the century.

As I sat in the English class I, my god was given a book to read by another dyslexic William Shakespeare. Romeo and Juliet honestly why couldn't it be called Juliet and Juliet at least I could try to read it. Juliet flashes her tits over the balcony and Juliet two (meaning me) tries to climb up and grope her lesbian style. I would like to know what thee and thou is all about is it teenage slang for thou can't climb because I hast a gammy leg. Can't someone translate this crap into readable English, sorry mate you lost me on verse one, I read a line and wanted to top myself. I can't sit through an hour of this, I must think of a plan of escape. Perhaps the vomit routine might do it although my stomach is empty, perhaps a migraine, no I did that yesterday. Well here goes under the table fingers down the throat and result all over the desk and one of the bitches that threw water over me.

The teacher soon got me outside and I was back in the cubical calling Alf and Bert. I soon recovered and sat thinking of Mrs Cooper once more. I must confess I did enjoy her classes even though she taught history I could imagine we were in the Napoleonic wars together or in Tudor times. I washed my face and looked at myself in the mirror wondering what I would look like at the age of thirty. Older and wiser with a different hair style and image without being terrified by the school bell knowing it was for class or break time. I would love to walk down the corridors without fear of being bullied by other students.

I used to play sports like tennis, basketball or hockey but I had problems in the shower or changing rooms because of other girls. They would steal my clothes or slap me, or push me against a cold locker. I have always been bullied and I have to say no one has ever been able to understand me. Understanding Jodie must be a contest and the winner gets to go to Disney for three weeks, well at least I understand me, I think.

I am cursed with a duff brain and a boring personality that's my lot in life, I have no real friends, parents that don't care and teachers I don't understand. But life goes droning on like Mrs Hammond god bless the old trout. I suppose some people would say that I am being too hard on myself but if you are criticised too much you believe in your own mind that you are no good. If I were to describe my life at thirteen I would say crap, I can draw, paint and do incredible things with clay but it ends there.

It was at this point that I considered that's enough, I have been the subject of ridicule bullied beyond belief and so I took up martial arts. My favourite was kickboxing, my instructor said that I was champion material and he wanted me to go into contests. I have to say for a man he was nice and so kind, I built up mental and physical strength through him teaching me. He taught me how to control my emotions and channel it into my boxing, he demonstrated how to get rid of pent up frustration but then he never met Mrs Cooper. What a challenge that would be even for him if she joined his class he would have a permanent erection to deal with. God bless Mr George saveloy Sidwell so called because of his big sausage penis. If Mrs Cooper was in his class there would be no boxing only pole vaulting.

In cookery class we had a Mrs Totter with the most enormous arse ever, whenever she bent down to take something out of the oven we had a total eclipse of the sun or the moon shining. My god could she cook, she was a wonder with her pastry and roast chicken, she reminded me of a turkey with her fat arse waggling. Her chins dangled nicely down and her hair stuck up in the air, short red and sticky. I managed to bake cookies and cakes

Thinking about my family I must mention the formal dinners that my dear parents were so proud of, they used to invite their well to do friends to these functions. Some of them were so weird and had horrendous table manners, my god they were awful. People like Janet and Brian, Janet would slurp her soup and Brian chewed his food like a camel. His mouth went into the most amazing contortions and I swear I could see every item of food that he consumed over dinner in his mouth. Janet kept tooting like a Kangaroo with turrets, it was about as entertaining as watching an angry pussy spot burst. We were told to watch our manners and sit up at the table, bleeding hypocrites, why should we innocent creatures be subject to this torture every month. Its child cruelty of the highest order and not for the faint hearted, it needs a government health warning. Parent's guests are bad for your health, especially when they embarrass you with stupid remarks about how you look like this relative or that. Or pointing out your skin condition or the way you wear your hair it's simply oh my god how you can even comment you sag sacks. I think my parents must have chosen their friends from a circus full of freaks.

And as for parties well all of them appeared in one room like they had been kidnapped and brought to the house. My god all of them in one room, how can they be so cruel as to put us through that. I thought even the Spanish inquisition wasn't as bad as this; it's so amazing what they put us children through. One couple were small in stature and I remember my parents lecturing us on being careful what we said. Tact and diplomacy were the key words in this case. But isn't it the case that, the more you try to avoid saying anything the more you slip up. My father asked them if they wanted a short, I nearly died and this was followed by similar references to their stature. None of these remarks were meant to offend them, but they inevitably did as they came at them like a verbal machine gun. But despite the remarks they continued visiting my parents as if they love to be insulted, my god I can imagine them saying I don't come here to be insulted and my father replying well where do you usually go? But my parents were really sociable and kind, they were popular with many people. I really don't blame them for the way I turned out; after all I was a raving teenager who was out to avenge the world for my horrendous school days.

I have already discussed my desire for women and the closer that I got to puberty the worse it got. I did concentrate in the classes on sexual development but again nothing mentioned about Lesbianism so that was balls. Oh but did the lecturer go on about periods like it was the only thing in life that mattered. Describing the time of the month (or the monthly cycle) as the breaking away of the uterus wall and a rush of blood flowing out, or something like that. Why didn't she say it would happen in English class at 10.00am when I was sat relaxed and not wearing a sanitary pad, what a soft bitch?

I was so embarrassed and wanted the ground to open and swallow me up. I wonder how many women have had accidents like that, god I nearly bled to death right there and even the boys nearly fainted it was like a massacre. My god you would think I could have had some sort of warning, for instance a bell ringing from down below or buzzer.

Apart from the near death experience I was shocked by how quick by breasts developed from tiny hills to mountains and not to mention the pubic hair, which grew like a thorn bush, both armpits were also blessed with the bush. Suddenly I was a woman its official the evidence was visible and even my body shape had altered into more curvy hips. Naturally this didn't happen overnight but over a few years I was now reaching sixteen and looking back at my early teens wondering how I survived. The bullying continued but the gangs were targeting new blood I was left to the hardcore bullies who concentrated their energies on the strong survivors.

The bullies reminded me of my embarrassing period in the English class by finding a sanitary towel and covering it with tomato sauce leaving it in my desk draw. Then making me know that it was there with subtle hints and innuendos very mature of them. I remember standing naked looking at my new body in a full-length mirror at my front and then the back. I touched my breasts and rubbed my nipple until they went hard, it was like someone had given me a new toy to play with. Here is your new body Jodie. I was also fascinated with my pussy, it was a new discovery and exciting to touch, I soon mastered the art of masturbation and enjoyed this immensely. I used to watch my fellow pupils in the shower and wonder what they would look like when they developed fully. I watched Television and movies and got turned on by the latest celebrities, women of course, my god they were gorgeous. I was entering a new world and loving it, all I desired was here before me and Mrs Cooper was at the top of my list. A sex goddess in my own classroom, my god I loved that lady and wanted her for my own. I was mature now that I had reached puberty so I could effectively be with her and we could have a thing going, my god dream on Jodie.

The puberty thing led its natural course to self-discovery as my friends and I shared over an ice cool milk shake and sweet doughnut. We were in a local cafe enjoying each other's company when the subject of sex, boys and girls came up. I had already indicated my desire for women and so Rachel asked me about my interests in the female form, she was as subtle as a flying mallet asking me the question 'Are you gay?'

"Well what do you think" I replied sharply

"Oh shit Jodie I didn't know" Rachel replied embarrassed on hearing the answer.

"My god Rachel you must have known" I said staring her right in the face.

"No honestly I didn't" Rachel said innocently.

"But all the things I said before, you must have picked up clues" I said trying to explain

"So how long have you known Jodie?" Rachel continued

"Since my body started changing I suppose" I said looking down onto my and pointing to my breasts.

I already knew about my sexuality and gender orientation, I was a female but had no interest in males, the male form to me was revolting and about attractive as cow shit. I wanted to experience sex with men just to prove the point. So I arranged to date a boy from school who I knew had a little experience with women in others words a male slag. John Green was anything but green he was said to be the hottest lover in school and I was the one to have sex with him convince him that I loved him and dump him. I was called the black widow spider because a black widow spider makes love with the male then will destroy him. I was right of course the most boring experience of my life and not worth returning to in a hurry. I don't rock to cock no way; I would rather have a donut with jam or cream. Of course I never really let on that I was gay just thrived on humiliating poor John, he became a right wanker of course.

My first female sexual experience was with a girl called Katie Barnes god bless her, we made out in the drama room. The front door was locked and we crept into the room via the stage from the main hallway. We had not intended to make love as we were just exploring looking for costumes to wear for a school production later that year. Well never the less we performed although I cannot go into detail, its up to your imagination.

After this event we regularly went to the same place and enjoyed lesbian sex in the same way. I knew then that I never ever wanted to be straight and that my future would be with women not men. I had always desired women but had never dipped my cherry before and so hadn't experienced the wonders of same sex relationships. My future was equally as colourful but that another story and there is much more to tell about my rebellious life. I regret few things in my life and I must say we all make love differently that's what makes a colourful world.

My schooling continued with very little problems I struggled through my classes due to dyslexia, no one helped of course. My parents despaired at my school reports and questioned me about my behaviour. I had a attitude but didn't care because I got no support and was expected to cope with subjects despite my disability. My teachers concentrated on the bright pupils and fuck the rest, so I continued in my own sweet way. My god no one understands Jodie or ever will, I am just crap under their shoes and people don't give a fuck about me. Jodie the no nobody and Jodie the troublemaker forget my achievements in art or my amazing ideas. I was fed up of existing in a classroom full of time wasters and rebels and I wanted to fit in somewhere. I had wondered what it must be like being in a gang and not being picked on as an individual, I would be protected for once and not expected to defend myself. I would belong to a group of people and share their life style and learn new things from them.

Camp trips had to be the highlight of my schooling, whoever created the idea of camping I could kiss them. Each year pupils would be chosen for their academic achievements or good behaviour in class, guess which category I went under. Well it was the good behaviour of course; at least it was for the duration of the year when I might be chosen. We travelled on the coach and I sat next to my friend Rachel as usual, my dishy best mate. We had just set off when I heard the sound of someone vomiting, my god the smell was revolting, I could not enjoy my small bar of chocolate with someone having a hughy behind me. The moment was lost and I had let my chocolate melt through my fingers as I waited for her to stop.

On the journey to the camp all I could think of was Rachel's body especially her legs, I thought to myself my god how can such a lovely body be wasted on a straight girl. I wish she was gay and then I could have my wicked way with her in our tent. At this moment I reverted my thoughts to the countryside at the roving hills and sparkling lake scenes so shapely just like Rachel, my god I am at it again with my perverse thoughts. Shit I hope the camp trip does not affect me, I must stay focused on something else or I am going to regret what I could potentially do. The fact that I am gay doesn't matter but to hit on my best friend my god that would be the cardinal sin.

We arrived on camp fairly late considering both the teachers and the driver professed to know the way. They had a navigation system and a map so how did they go wrong, oh don't tell me males created both of them and males were trying to understand them. Who is sexist my god it's a wonder we ever got there, the word dick head springs to mind. Never the less we made it in one piece, then came the putting up of the tents in the dark and the cussing and swearing that went on was worse than going down a mineshaft or entering a factory. It was all shit, fuck and bollocks and that was the clean stuff, my god I have never heard so much foreign language even in France. Once the tents were up (helped by a few torches of course) we were all told to assemble outside the tents while we were allocated our tents. Of course we got the usual lecture about behaving and sticking to the school rules, this meant no smoking, drinking, swearing, stealing and doing anything to upset the other pupils or teachers. Yeah like that's going to happen, like we will not obey any of their crappy rules, we are here to have fun in life.

Nobody mentioned sex I wonder why, is it because Mr Harvey fancied the knickers off Mrs Lewis from science, Old Harvey was one of the geography teachers who wanted to explore most female teachers contours and knock them off their equator. He was just a saucy bastard who had a permanent volcano in his trousers; you could tell when he had an erection when he walked sideways. Talk about tent pole he could jack up a car with that mother, I pity Mrs Lewis my god she was in for a challenge. Talk about the cave of wonders, he would need a good light to go potholing there.

It was actually day two when he got his wicked end away, How gullible does he think we are, my god he went into the Mrs Lewis's tent just after midnight, Rachel and myself stayed awake to hear her enter his tent and then we crept up and fastened the tent flaps with safety pins, then by five O'clock we heard her struggling to get out. I must say they must think we are deaf as they give it throttle in the sack, moaning and groaning do they think we are so daft that we think it's the wildlife. And what would their respective partners think of them acting this way on camp. The following nights he was flapping her tent flaps and this time he put his foot in a cow pat, god the smell followed him everywhere for days. Funnily enough Mrs Lewis didn't visit him for days afterwards.

On camp we got involved with competitive sports such as tennis, rounders and tug of war. Here came my big moment as I played rounder's

I couldn't catch a cold even worse a ball, for me to be fielding was a complete wonder and disaster in one. I stood there watching the play and then low and behold my moment came, as the ball flew in the air and descended right above me. I cupped my hands and it was like slow motion as the ball landed right in the palm of my hands. Glory I had actually caught the fucking ball, my god me actually catching the ball and everyone applauded me. I was living the moment right here right now.

Well I have a new name for Mrs Lewis; I shall call her either Mrs Scabby knickers or sticky knickers which ever suits her most. She had certainly seen action in her merry little life as she made her way through the male teachers, I am truly grateful that she don't like woman as well. The anorexic nymphomaniac would have a field day with everyone.

The remainder of the camp trip was like carry on camping without the carry on crew. The showers were cubicles with holes in the walls with the male shower rooms next door, oh now where have I seen that before, yes in a scene from carry on camping with Sid James looking through the hole at naked women like Barbara Winsor. But I was prepared with towels and such to cover the holes or a good deodorant to sting the eyes. No purvey men were seeing my naked body or female bits.

Mr Lawrence the religious teacher was with us on the camping trip, he joined us for spiritual guidance. To be perfectly frank I would have preferred a nun with a dirty habit or even the pope in drag. Mr Lawrence was a soft tit, who hated lesbians and thought that it was a sin for the same sex people cohabitate and have sexual intercourse together. I considered him to be lost up his own rectum and suggested that he read the beano instead of the bible. A child's comic would provide him with more insight than what he referred to as god's word, bless the dozy bullock. I was often criticized by Christians and Muslims alike who clearly did not understand anything about Lesbianism, what about reproduction they asked? "Fuck that, what about my own state of mind" I replied.

The only other things I remember from camp were the flatulence and the horrendous food leading up to this condition. Some of the pupils could strike up a band with the farting, it's a wonder that we didn't have explosions all over the camp when they sat by the camp fires to sing. We had burnt offerings almost every night which was said to be a barbecue, I am sure that the Australians didn't introduce this sort of barbecue to England. The songs were boring too what the hell is a ging gang goolie or whatever they were singing was it a tentacle that hung funny.

So we went to bed and during the night we heard the sound of the wind howling through the trees and the odd bang. It sometimes sounded like whistling and explosions. My god we are under attack from al-Qaeda or some other terrorist air raid, maybe even the Russians. Rachel jumped into my bed and I must confess I was glad she did, speaking from a completely selfish point of view. I could feel her trembling body close to mine and I swear she had wet herself with fear, but I wasn't prepared to let her go as I was comforting her. She was convinced that we were under attack and were sure to die, imagine ending our lives here and not even experiencing full on snogging. It was at this point that we heard thunder followed by a heavy rain pour as the heavens really opened thrashing at the tent. Rachel and I sighed with relief and fell off to sleep in each other's arms, by the morning I had turned my back to Rachel and she had clung to my back. I could feel Rachel's breath on the back and my god I felt horny, I had turned so not to get so turned on by her body. She suddenly woke up and climbed across me to look outside the tent.

"Come and look at this" she invited me to look outside.

"My god" I exclaimed as I looked around the camp only to notice that all the tents but ours had blown over.

It looked a complete mess with loads of tent poles and canvases everywhere, but where were the pupils and teachers?

We later discovered that they had all slept in an ex army billet that we would have used had we not gone camping. We had a good mountain tent and so we were comfortable, safe and dry, unlike our poor unfortunate friends. I have to confess to feeling exhilarated for more reasons than none, after all some of these were bullies from school. This is what I consider rough justice and as the religious teacher Mr Lawrence would say god moves in mysterious ways. I call it rough justice although some of the teachers and pupils were not so bad.

Moving sweetly on in a fashion that I had become accustomed to I began to really get annoyed with the bullies. I was always getting in trouble with other girls or teachers although I earned respect when I dumped John. I was termed as lazy, thick and no good so much that I was beginning to believe it myself. But what everyone didn't believe was that I wanted to get on in school and be academic but my dyslexia was holding me back.

Mrs Cooper helped me but one day I was given the news that she had tragically died in a road traffic accident. I was in shock I couldn't eat, drink or sleep my world was turned upside down.

I headed for the toilets and threw my ring up, suddenly the bowl became huge and my head seemed small inside it. I clung hold of the sides and felt dizzy. At that moment I heard a voice outside taunting me challenging me to a fight, we were near the gymnasium and I thought this was it my chance to finish the bullying.

Donna welsh was built like a sumo wrestler big, mean and ugly with only one brain cell floating in her head. I could hear the bitch shouting abuse at me and banging at the cubicle door.

"Hey black widow come out here and get laid lesbian bitch" Donna shouted loudly in a mean menacing voice.

I opened the door and stared her in the eyes, her pig like eyes looked back at me with pure hate written across her expression.

We both walked into the gym and two other women each accompanied her holding a bat as a weapon.

"I hear you don't like me bitch" Donna said angrily

"I never said that" I replied confused

"Are you fucking calling me a liar" Donna continued

"No" I made it clear I wanted no trouble "I want no trouble"

"What's that noise, I hear a mouse squeaking" Donna looked back at her friends for support.

"Me too" said one of the gang

"Don't tread on the mouse girls" Donna said sarcastically

"I'm no mouse" I replied bravely or stupidly I suppose

"Sorry you squeaked girl, fuck she squeaked" Donna suddenly hit me in the stomach with her bat.

I fell to the ground holding my stomach one of the women went to hit me with her bat when Donna stopped her

"This bitch is mine" Donna said watching me trying to get up

"I said I don't want trouble" I told them again remembering the self control that my instructor taught me.

Again Donna hit me this time in the ribs, this time I fell backwards but remained standing as she thumped me in the nose.

I felt the blood trickle down and onto the floor and knew by now I had to defend myself. Donna rushed forward to attack again this time I swerved to one side and she hit the wall with the force of her body. I quickly turned and kicked her in the small of her back and she fell like a sack of potatoes. One of the other women raced to her defence and was immediately knocked to the ground with a kick to the throat. The other woman tried a pathetic punch, which didn't even connect, and I simply kicked her legs from under her and delivered a blow to her stomach.

Donna tried to get up but I thumped her repeatedly on the face and drop kicked her in the chest and she rapidly returned to the ground.

At that point the teacher came in clapping slowly

"Oh very good Jodie Brown, excellent for your school record" the teacher went on "So what do you do for an encore, break bones?"

I was so surprised at her attitude considering I was defending myself

"But miss I was ganged up on they were trying to beat me up" I said knowing that I was on to a loser.

"Looks like it Jodie, I think you beat them up" She said almost smiling

I really think she thought I was in the right but could not admit it.

At this point my parents were called into school and the facts were so twisted not even a judge would be able to fathom out the truth. My parents were certainly shocked at my behaviour but then they didn't quite understand my dyslexia or in fact why they had me in the first place from what I could see both sat in the office not saying a word. Neither mother or father gave me eye contact, I was just listening to the whole circus wondering why I bothered defending myself in the first place.

The head of school gave a nice speech about self-control and how I apparently beat up three girls and used kickboxing to do this. The only one who actually believed me was George my instructor; he was not surprised at the story as I related it to him, according to George self defence can be a case of you defending yourself but the attackers injuring themselves through their own efforts to hurt you. But unfortunately that didn't help this situation and my school record.

"I have something to say" I announced proudly

Everyone looked at me as if I had two heads, not one person actually cared what I thought, but I continued anyway.

"When I was seven and being bullied who helped me and as the years went on did I get help with dyslexia, no I didn't, and then I came to this poxy school and was I bullied again yes I was and was I helped, no I wasn't, so the day I fight back its all sympathy to the other poor girls but me I get punished. My god where's the justice in that?" After I given my elaborate speech for justice the room was silent I felt that I had given my all and that everyone would sympathize or even empathize but nothing. It was as if I had simply farted and not apologised for my actions, wasted gas from the ass a pointless exercise for me.

However I did gain the respect of the school pupils after this day, I was conscious of the golden rule of not getting the other girls in trouble by telling the head teacher about their antics. Donna never approached me again and wanted me to join her gang, naturally I refused that treat and continued with my artwork without any further problems. I realised bullies just needed to know that they were not going to get away with hurting other pupils and that was good enough reason to punch the lights out of the bullies. The secret was to find the leader of a gang or ringleader and beat them up first, like skittles find the strongest and hit that and watch the others fall. Simple logic that even the dumbest person could work out, I was considered thick, but I proved that I was knowledgeable at times.

I hated being called out of class to the special lesson for dyslexia or other learning difficulties. It was quite obvious where we were going, when the special needs teacher blurted it out in class. My god, why didn't she just blow a trumpet and announce it properly like,

"Jodie, can you please come to your dyslexic class!" Honestly how discrete is that and my form teacher didn't help as she pointed me out so that all the other pupils would see me. My god I wanted to die on the spot or hope the ground would open up and swallow me whole. My entire school days were embarrassing for one reason or another, poor Jodie the one no one understood or the dyslexic lesbian.

OH TO BE A GOTH

The next phase in my life happened by accident as I pointed out I never wanted to be in any gang, I never agreed to gangs or the problems that went along with them. Usually a gang hanging around a street corner meant trouble and could look menacing for others.

At first it was like experimenting with make up, mainly black, with a subtle application of rouge to give a pale effect to the skin which also covered up the present acne problem. Then the eye liner and mascara with a hint of purple or blue on the eye lids and surrounding area. With black eye brows and black lip stick, I had already dyed my hair black and dressed in black with a black necklace and black nail varnish I was almost ready for the schools Halloween party.

I wore a black skirt and black tights with stylish boots to match and a black-laced blouse; looking back I was a dead ringer for Morticia from the Adams family. Such a scary sight to behold but fitting for a Halloween party, which was arranged by the school for a get together of students, teachers and parents. It was well organised I must admit but guess who's parents didn't attend? Yes surprise mine god bless them.

I reached the school hall and noticed quite a few people dressed for the occasion. It was most impressive inside like a horror movie film set such as Van Helsing with a long buffet like Harry Potter's Hogwarts School. It was a good turn out the hall was packed with witches, devils and vampires all feasting. But something was wrong not all the people fitted in seemingly slightly out of place, particularly one gentleman who stood out with his strange top hat and long black coat. He even acted oddly as he walk around with a blonde woman who seemed to frown at everyone.

He finally stood in front of me and eyed me up and down, then looked at his companion.

"Marsha my dear I think we have found a Goth" He said confidently

Marsha didn't seem impressed gazing at me and then brushing her blonde hair back with her hand. She was dressed very much like me but had some sort of flower in her hair.

"Well be polite and say hello" He insisted

"Hello" She said reluctantly

"My name is snake, and who might you be?" Snake asked

I looked at his rather long nose and narrow face, I remember thinking he was skinny enough to be a snake, long and thin.

"I am Jodie" I said hesitantly

"But people call you black widow" He said looking at Donna across the hallway.

"I have been known as the black widow for certain reasons" I smiled at him because I knew what he was referring to.

"Poor Johnny got his tail cut off with you the spider who eats his lover after making love, I like it". Snake smiled cunningly.

I suppose Snake could come across creepy at first, but he had a lovable side to him. He had a dry sense of humour and loved the mystical side of life; he was very much into Gothic art and music.

As for Marsha she was very much in love with Snake and was so jealous of me, she detected an attraction between Snake and myself I was merely fascinated by him but he was attracted to me sexually. Marsha refused to speak to me from this day forward; she also had a cruel streak in her and would often use it to push away possible admirers of Snake.

Snake was almost like a Messiah, people often followed him and would do anything he said, they latched on to his every word and believed that he possessed magical powers. His disciples were all around him most of the time I met them later when I visited their hang out as he called it.

It was a old disused church or at least the ruins which lay close to the city.

I left the party with Snake, Marsha and a strange little man called shady he was called this because he liked to walk in shaded areas and he was so quiet. Once in the ruins I met Juicy lucy a blonde bimbo who was always giggling Mash a fat boy who loved mash potatoes, Clay who was a big hard man who never smiled. Fudge was a fat girl who was always eating, Drab was a girl who dressed more plainly and came out with boring things. The rest were not even mentionable and easily forgotten, all followed Snake and listened to his words of wisdom.

All I heard initially was Goth music being played constantly and the odd smell of cat piss which indicated someone was on the wacky backy or cannabis. Snake approached me after attending the church a few nights

"If you're with us you need to prove it" He looked serious

"What do you mean" I asked not knowing what to expect

"Oh like an initiation into our gang" He replied looking at the others

"What do I do?" I said worried to death that he might get me to eat a live toad or sacrifice a lamb.

Instead it was decided that I do three tasks to prove I am loyal to the Goth gang and to Snake, the first was to go into a confession box and urinate in it, the second to steal fruit from a market stall, and finally to cut my hand and share my blood with Snake. He had a thing about blood, which I never fully understood it was most strange.

My first task had to be the worst ever I entered a catholic church and the gang kept look out as I checked the door hoping it was locked and that I could be saved from the humiliation of this deed. Alas it was open and so I went in nervously and immediately dropped my knickers and urinated on the floor, it seemed to last for ages and although it was dark I swear I could see the shiny wet floor. I was soon out of there and actually saw urine coming out of the box that had to be evidence of my deed. A priest went in soon after with a catholic woman and came straight out in discussed. My second task was simple stealing fruit I took a pile of oranges off a fruit stall and ran swiftly, a man ran after me but he was too slow and I escaped unharmed. The third task was painful and bizarre as I cut my hand with a knife and Marsha was asked to cut hers, we were made to join hands and Snake captured our blood in the palm of his hand and licked it off like a vampire.

I was often curious about the plans made by Snake as he was clearly not singing from the same hymn sheet as me, he definitely had a slate missing off the roof and that concerned me greatly. I often wondered whether or not he was on medication for some sort of mental illness. Not being an expert I could not put my finger on what exactly was wrong with him. But I had joined the gang for a reason, for protection and that was my excuse for what it was worth. The weird eccentricities displayed by Snake added to an unsettled feeling that I had from the start, I suppose that I was curious to see whether or not he was truly insane or just bizarre.

We often went for night walks especially on foggy nights, we were like silhouettes in the lamp lit streets immerging like figures from time. Imagine a Dickens movie like Oliver Twist or something like Sherlock Holmes, it was as if we had entered a time warp and were living in Victorian England. Goth was cool but I felt uneasy, as we seemed to up set a lot of people with our antics. For anyone who saw us I should imagine we looked quite menacing, wearing our black attire and acting strangely.

As Goths we were devoted to our music and life style I was living with Juicy Lucy for my sins and my god I was paying dearly for that. She was one annoying bitch with her silly laugh and dozy ways it was only one step better than living with wanking Tom and tormenting Gary. What we lesbians have to put up with. Masturbation was all right but not when you got disturbed doing it, after all I once caught Tom cranking his pole and he caught me weaving the basket, so I guess we were evens. Well its normal and I bet even royalty does it at times, there must be royal tossers

Somewhere.

Snake suddenly spun round his long coat flowed as he did so; he had a look of devilment in his eyes.

"Lets have some fun" He announced

He looked around him and smiled "It's a perfect evening for fun"

When he acts like this you can expect problems, he was bored and needed excitement. Everyone looked to him for inspiration after all he was the dark messiah and what he said was to be happened.

Drab looked at the others with a vacant expression on his face

"Are you with us Drab?" Snake asked

"Just thinking" Drab replied

"Well don't fucking strain your head Drab" Marsha said teasing him

"Why do you keep picking on Drab?" I asked Marsha

"Keep your nose out widow" Marsha said poking me in the shoulder

I was so angry at her attitude towards me and constantly picking on Drab.

"Why what you gonna do if I don't Marsha?" I said challenging her

"Just keep on black Widow and you will see" Marsha said pointing at me

"Now girls lets be nice ok" Snake advised

"My god Marsha what have you got against me?" I asked her in order to bring our problems out in the open.

"I don't know I just don't like you" Marsha admitted

"But we all need to get on we are like family" Snake chipped in.

"So no bitchiness he went on".

"I agree" Drab said

"You would you freak because you fancy her, but she's gay brain ache"

Marsha ought to have been called Snake as she had so much venom

That was the last straw I heard her remarks towards Drab and lost my temper, I charged at Marsha and pushed her.

She stepped back at the same time and landed me a cunning blow to the face. I thought my nose was going to explode as her fist made contact I fell back and Marsha saw her opportunity and jumped on top of me. Normally I would enjoy this but Marsha was one hateful lady and she had the advantage being such a crafty madam. Marsha was hitting my head on the pavement until I managed to knee her in the back, then I did what girls do best grabbed her hair and pushed her off me. I then returned a punch to the nose and a thump to the chest. We seemed to be rolling around the pavement for ages until Snake and a few others stopped us.

We both stood with blood on our faces staring at each other with hatred in our eyes. Snake was pacing up and down and so disappointed with us and the others just remained quiet. We were still being held while Snake suddenly slapped us both on the face in temper.

"This does not happen ever, you are both fucking idiots" He then noticed that he had blood from both off us on his fingers and sucked it off.

"Let's go back to the church" He insisted.

I had a nightmare that very same evening; I fell asleep and began dreaming of vampires. Snake appeared at the church and was making eyes at me; he put me in a trance and my god I was under his spell. It was horrid suddenly he had fangs and was sucking the blood from my neck. I went white and collapsed onto the church alter, where other vampires like Marsha also bit me and sucked my blood. I woke up in a cold sweat and staring into the darkness, hoping it was just a dream. It felt so real and Snake made a good vampire, his lust for blood made me think so and as for Martha well her wild behaviour was evident in my dream. I came to life as a vampire and walked through a graveyard, I travelled through mist and felt totally alone. Other vampires who floated around me in mid air, each one looked magnificent in their costumes suddenly joined me and their fangs were shining in the moonlight. A loud sound echoed in the darkness and we had vampire hunters pursuing all of us. I found it difficult to fly properly and felt something pierce my side, I fell to the ground and a ugly man held up a sharp steak to my chest. He drew back and then forced it into my chest and I awoke from the dream petrified.

I remained with the Goth gang for two years, going to the church having parties and listening to the Goth music. I must say I did enjoy most of my time with them, until I reached the age of eighteen. In fact I even celebrated my eighteenth birthday with them in Gothic style. Snake remained the leader of the gang and Marsha remained by his side, he became stranger than ever. Marsha was always jealous of Snake and I, she hated the attention that he gave me although I am a lesbian; Marsha thought I was a bi sexual. Snake also attempted to kiss me and made a fuss of me, she even heard him discussing how fed up he was with her and her clinging ways. This made Marsha more determined to get rid of me out of the gang; she never liked me and was obviously planning this for some time. We had many verbal fights but tried to keep the peace for the sake of the gang. But even some of the gang members were finding other interests and were hardly ever together. People were starting to mistrust Snake and no longer think of him as some sort of messiah, he had lost his credibility since his strange behaviour.

Marsha left the gang for a while, but returned trying to rekindle her love for Snake. But Snake still tried to come on to me and rejected her pursuits, this angered her and she continued to plan her revenge on me. Then on what I would consider the worst night of my life Marsha sat in the church beside Snake, she was looking a little sheepish with a guilty look on her face. It was as if she had done something wrong.

The moon was full and Snake was particularly agitated pacing up and down in the church. I noticed someone standing near him who I had not seen before; he was wearing a leather jacket and looked unshaven with a front tooth missing. I approach them hoping to find out what was happening but they were being very secretive. I asked Clay about him but all he could give me was his name 'Weed' and that he was into drugs. I must confess drugs certainly were not my scene and I was not about to try them. So the presence of Weed didn't please me, I was contemplating leaving them at this point but Clay gave me some cider and I foolishly stayed. I was relaxed drinking my cider god knows how much I had but I felt merry and I found that even Drab was interesting to talk to. My god I felt good at this point, but I remember saying to someone that I had a headache probably due to the cider. Someone passed me some tablets and I felt as if I was flying through clouds.

I think that it must have been Marsha looking back at the turn of events. Soon after this we went out and Snake was calmer although he seemed to be on a mission, he beckoned us on into the night under the light of the full moon. Snakes eyes were red and his pupils were dilated he was acting strange, out of character even for him. I think we were all high on something I remember being confused and my body didn't seen as if it belonged to me. Fudge seemed breathless clinging hold of her fat as she walked down the street. It was like looking at a dark marsh mellow and Juicy was dancing in the street.

Suddenly we met a rival gang across the street, they were rockers dressed in leather jackets and jeans. They began taunting us shouting abuse one of the Goths shouted back abuse but added a few choice words of his own. This cause tension between both gangs and we were soon in a fight. Fists were flying, kicking and brawling in the street. This is when Marsha seized her opportunity and began kicking one of the girls in the other gang behind me. She managed to get her on the ground and continued punching and kicking her. I tried to stop her but felt something hard hitting my head and I fell to the ground dazed. Marsha saw her chance and began kicking me; it was awful I lay next to the other girl who looked badly beaten. Suddenly I heard police sirens and before long both the gangs disbursed and both the girl and I were alone. I stood up and looked at her, I wanted to help her, but I was handcuffed and she was being helped by the police an ambulance came and took her away and guess who got blamed for her beating. Yes I did, although I was dazed and confused I could beat up a girl and do such amazing things. I could feel blood on my face and my ribs felt broken as I ducked my head down in order to get into the police car. I remember hearing the girls name mentioned Joanna, so I repeated it to myself so that I wouldn't forget it. I felt so bad about her although it wasn't my fault; I suppose I should have made more effort to save her. If my head wasn't so fucked up I could have helped her, but things were so insane and those tablets were no doubt ecstasy. So

I am a druggy and maybe a murderer, in a Goth gang and god knows what else.

Following the tragic attack on the young girl Joanna who by some miracle survived, I was held in the local police station, I was sat in a cell looking at the horrid walls and iron door which I had previously seen on television in cop shows. I never thought for one moment that I would be in one, next comes the interrogation. The strong light in the face and asked to talk and reveal all, my god will I fuck. Although the heating is on it still seems freezing, colder than that church that I was in, oh to be a Goth. I still think of Mrs Cooper and being back at school those moments of being bullied and my glory day striking back. My god I defended myself that day, no fucker was going to bully me forever. You can only take so much then blow, give the bastards everything you've got, don't let them beat you.

Oh here we go the doors being unlocked and footsteps; of course it takes an army to escort me to the interrogation room, my god sad bastards. They led me to a room with a great big mirror, probably two was so they could psycho analyse me and say what a poor child led into this situation, deprived of parental love and all that bollocks. My god I do love these places, sitting on a plastic chair with a wooden table and strangers in the room. A woman say beside me and introduced herself as my legal representative called Kathy, my god she was ugly, everybody has the right to be ugly but she abused the privilege. She had obviously fell out the ugly tree and hit every branch on the way down.

One of the officers sat staring at me like I was a freak, in the end I couldn't help myself I gave him a visual sign with my index finger basically saying screw you pal. It didn't go down to well I guess he wasn't getting any from his misses and took it out on me. It was a case of good cop bad cop the policewoman was nicer and I do love a woman in uniform, they are so superior and domineering. I must confess I am a submissive lesbian who likes to be told what to do sexually. So back to the interrogation with the policeman with a big nose postman pat with an attitude. He questioned me about my actions and reminded me of my school report, the one-day that I defended myself and I get this shit. He leaned forward almost in my face I could almost lick his nose, or tickle all the strands of hair growing out of it.

"So why join a gang?" He asked

Before I had chance to answer he was in with the next question

"Is it because you thrive on beating girls up?" He said with a smirk

"No I fucking well don't I was the one being bullied at school and who helped me then? No one so I had to defend myself or continued being bullied not like you arse holes would understand that" I said in anger.

"Wow temper Jodie" He said with his hands up

Even the female officer looked at him with discussed

She cleared her throat and began talking to me softly but with authority

"Jodie we realise its been difficult for you, but beating up a girl is no answer, why do that?"

"I guess I wanted to be noticed in the gang as they protected me"

I completely lost it, I was lying so the gang didn't get into trouble I was actually protecting Marsha, knowing the bitch wouldn't defend me

In any way. The rest of interview went reasonably well I just kept quiet shed a few crocodile tears and then waited for the outcome.

I was an hour in the interview room waiting for my parents to arrive, which was an agonising time when they came in and almost blanked me. I was clearly invisible as the police spoke to them in length about my behaviour. All I could do was sit there kicking my feet against the table with my boots on and thinking this is the first time that I have seen my parents in months. My father made an exhibition of himself saying how he had provided for the family and I was the only problem in his life, yes bull shit dad. Mother just broke down in tears and gave it the woe is me treatment. I suppose this is parenthood, not for me I am glad that I am a lesbian no kids and no hassle, apart from now of course.

The end result meant that I had to go to prison for a short time, on my fathers request he wanted me punished and was determined to let them do this. The judge said that I was to be made an example of to deter other gangs from doing the same harm to an individual. The jury sat looking at me as if I had two heads and came out of a circus, I dressed Goth so what get over it. I was going to explain that not all Goths are in gangs and fight but who would believe me, these chosen people the jury from all walks of life most of them didn't even want to be there. They didn't care about me just got their day off work and got paid for sending me down.

I still see my fathers face as he shouted send her down and punish her for what she's done and I suppose if the tables were turned I would have done the same thing. I understand that he was actually heart broken having to make that decision based on the evidence provided, I really don't blame him at all. I might even say the next years did me good because I became stronger and more determined to fight my disability called dyslexia.

Jodie continued to explain to Faith how things happened little knowing the battle that was occurring in the spirit world between Faith and Fiona mainly. The fallen angels led by Satan were hoping to capture Jodie's soul, Jodie was walking right into their hands, she demonstrated this by her actions but Faith was determined to win. Faith could see the good in Jodie by the way she was with others, trying to help the weak ones in the gang. But Fiona was behind Marsha being so bad and would be influencing those in prison.

Jodie continued her story about prison life although Faith knew all about it observing from afar.

I was taken to a women's open prison for six months and my god was that rough, I was stripped which was nice and searched. Then examined by a doctor for my fitness and her pleasure no doubt purvey bitch. I was then taken inside to meet other prisoners and officers, some were definitely butch lesbians and my gaydar was on checking them over. This is when I first met Fiona a female prisoner who was worse than Marsha, she was more mean and jealous than she was. In fact she was pure evil. She hated everybody at times, She wanted to harm everyone, but even she could be nice if she wanted something.

I was assigned to a job in the prison on laundry as Chinese washerwoman calling me 'wha wen Wong', a question I always ask myself. I visited all areas of the prison collecting washing from the beds and prisoners; I must say some bedding was disgusting. It was a case of blood, piss, other body fluids and shit, sometimes-sweaty towels and sheets. Often you could match the bedding with the prisoner just looking at each one and thinking my god I am in for a treat today. I did my time at that prison and knew about it blood sweat and years I called it, with no time off for good behaviour. Some young girls were less hard than me and got sucked into the meanest bunch of hard-core prisoners ever known; they were bait on the hook no danger.

I lay in my cell each night reflecting on my past I was a mere eighteen year old spending my time in prison bored out of my tiny head. I did wonder how that girl had been getting on that I allegedly beat up. I did feel bad that I was once being bullied and now I am classed as a bully it was not what I wanted. Now I was classed as a young offender and had a criminal record doing time in affect for Marsha. I met an odd woman with fair hair and small nose called Fiona who seemed to just stare at me and make me feel uneasy.

To be honest I wanted to punish myself but I couldn't quite think of how I could do this effectively, then I cam up with a plan. If I could get someone else to do this I would be satisfied in my own mind that I was being punished and could sleep at night without having a conscience. T he way to do this was to approach the top dog and insult her, this would lead to her beating me up and therefore I was punished. This was possibly a strange way to get punished but effective if I wanted to be free from guilt. Fiona made me feel guilty by saying that I should punish myself for such crimes and suffer any punishment bestowed on myself. She even indicated that I should consider suicide taking myself out of this wicked world.

I planted the seed by making it known that I thought Doggie was a fat tart with nothing better to do with her time than shagging fresh new girls. It worked a treat telling the right people such as Fiona, the gossip reached her in seconds and she was after me. I headed for the shower and one of the women alerted doggie, I was in the shower when she arrived looking angry and mean.

"Well what's this then pretty girl?" Doggie began

"Oh, hi there" I shouted bravely

"What are you staring at, do you like what you see" Doggie said posing.

"No I don't like butch women" I said looking her up and down

"What did you say lesbo?" Doggie asked

"You heard you're too butch for me, excess fat and all that" I was shaking with fear inside as I said this.

"Hey girls why don't we teach this gay bitch a lesson?" Doggie said addressing her friends

"Perhaps she prefers me" said one of her friends covered in tattoos

"I must admit your dishy" I said admiring her tattoos

"Nah she wants it rough so lets give it her rough" Doggie said grabbing my hair and pulling her out of the shower, each girl began to slap me, but I wanted punishment not pleasure.

"Pass me that broom Debbie" Doggie said without taking her eyes off me.

She asked them to pin me down and I seriously thought she was going to insert the broom into my virginals. She held it tight and asked them to hold me still, then she stopped and laughed really loud, I was bracing myself for the worst and thought my worst nightmare was about to happen.

But she broke the stick on her knee and threw it away, and then in temper she started punching me hard in the stomach and face. Each blow was like being hit with a rock and I felt myself getting weaker and weaker until I collapsed. The floor was a mess with soapsuds and my blood, I crawled to the place where I had left my clothes and tried to focus but my eye was closing. The next thing I remember was my friend jasmine helping me back to my cell. My god my face was a mess and I could hardly walk I swear I had broken ribs.

Fiona was behind every attack dropping down the poison each time making it obvious that she was the real instigator of all the trouble. After this Doggie and every other bully targeted me I was like flavour of the month, every problem was caused by me and I was getting slapped, punched and a subject of laughter it was worse than school for a while.

But I did go mad when my friend Jasmine got beat up she was so badly injured she ended up in the prison hospital. I was so angry I went after Doggie to teach her a lesson she would never forget.

I marched towards Doggies cell her friends Sue and Debbie were there guarding the door like 10 Downing street. One of them put her arm out to stop me and found herself on the floor in seconds holding her throat. So the other rushed forward and I drop kicked her in the stomach, and then punched her in the jaw. I remember shouting or screaming like a banshee as I entered Doggies cell, she knew I meant business as she was immediately on the defensive trying to attack me with a chair.

"Now bitch it's my turn" I shouted

I ploughed into her like a bull, firstly with a high kick to the chest and then without stopping I gave her one punch after another until she went down hard onto the ground. Debbie and Sue entered the cell but kept their distance from me as they tried picking Doggie up, I watched her chest rise so that I knew she was breathing then left the cell. Two prison wardens took me to the governor's office, but I was just given a warning and extra duties. Most of the time the wardens let you fight your own battles, as it was a tussle for power and survival of the fittest that's what prison is basically all about. Reform was just a buzzword branded about by the local goodie goodies that just wanted to be seen doing something for prisoners. No one fully understood peoples past lives and what made them commit crimes, the poverty and hardships of prisoners. Parents who were alcohols or drug addict what chance had any child got growing up in that kind of environment. Doggie was brought up with a schizophrenic mother and a violent drunken father; she just knew how to be a prostitute in order to survive. Pat was brought up to steal and it became a way of life to con people, she knew no other life. I was also amazed at the amount of dyslexic prisoners all went to school but slipped through the net struggling to survive in society. Either you form your own strategies to read and write or you just give in and blame society for your lack of education or in failing to acknowledge your disability.

Education was available in prison, but it was up to the individual to seek the courses and enrol, help was out their, if you made the effort to go and find out more. I was approached after the incident with Doggie and I took it, before long I was doing O 'levels in five subjects. Things were looking up after that day in the governor's office, but Fiona seemed to be the one causing all the trouble behind the scenes.

However later that day I was in the exercise yard, when Doggie approached me, she had a gang of women around her who formed around me in one big circle. A number of officers watched as Doggie moved forward towards me, no one else moved and the atmosphere was tense.

The prison wardens looked on but then appeared surprised as Doggie put out her hand in friendship even Fiona was shocked. I was very surprised and put out my hand to shake hers; she held my hand firmly and smiled.

"Few people have dared challenge me, no one has ever beaten me" Doggie said humbly

I could only smile back and listen to her

"Your one fucking brave lady" Doggie looked into my eyes

"I was merely defending myself" I admitted.

"Well you can certainly fight" Doggie said admiringly

At that the crowd dispersed.

"How did you learn to fight like that?" Doggie asked

"I had a good teacher, he taught me to defend myself" I explained

"So why did you let me beat you up in the shower?" Doggie asked confused

"I needed to be punished because I fucked up being in a gang" I wanted to tell her everything and why not she was hardly going to meet Marsha.

So I told her all about the Goth gang and my circumstances and to my surprise she was so sympathetic and understanding of my situation. Her advice to me was to seek education fight dyslexia like I fought her and make peace with my parents. I swore never again to misjudge people and I would also help anyone who needed it no matter who they were. Doggie admired my artwork and made me promise not just to pursue education but also to seek a career.

As things turned out it seems that Joanna the girl I allegedly beat up explained to the police that I was innocent and that Marsha was the guilty one who assaulted her. So I was officially vindicated and guess who was coming to jail and doing time for her crime? It was one other than Marsha. Yes I was to be released and she was coming in and serving twelve months for that and a further time for drug dealing. I was to be released but had no idea where I was going for the next six months. My parents wanted me back but I was not prepared to go home just yet. I was given the opportunity to work in a holiday camp with good references and a clean record. That at least was a start and I could think about my future while cleaning out chalets and having fun at a major holiday camp.

Jodie told Faith about Marsha and her reaction to seeing her again, the one that caused her so many problems in the past.

Marsha appeared in the prison and at that point I was being escorted out, we passed each other and I launched at her taking everyone by surprise. Two guards pulled me off her but not until I had punch her directly in the face. She was holding her face and blood was oozing through her fingers, she looked scared and was reluctant to retaliate, I was so angry at seeing her I decided to offer her a little verbal service.

"You fucking bitch, you nearly ruined my life" I said still being held

"Make her suffer girls, make her pay for what she has done".

Fiona observed in the background hoping to see Jodie make a mistake and batter the girl to death before her eyes, that way she would win her soul back from Faith.

Jodie spoke to Faith conveying her life after prison back in employment, she want Faith to know about her life after prison although Faith was fully aware of her movements virtually throughout her life. But never intervened until Faith was told that if she failed to help her that she would spend the rest of her life on earth as a human or a mortal being. Faith herself had made mistakes as a guardian angel so she was aware of Jodie's imperfections.

Jodie left the prison free and innocent of the crimes that she had been convicted of throughout her past.

"Am I bitter, am I fuck, whoops sorry Faith, I just wanted to move on and do something different. I needed a further break from the parents and the holiday camp seemed like a good place to go away and rethink my life. I was now more educated and perhaps more mature; I was almost a sensible woman" She told Faith.

Jodie began work at the holiday camp it was nice to wake up and smell the sea. Up early with my equipment consisting of a mop, bucket and rags armed to the teeth to clean chalets.

"My word I was going to scrub them chalets until they gleamed I planned to be the best scrubber in the camp. By that I don't mean a tart there were enough of them about drooling after the entertainers enough to make me vomit. I was there to have some fun and seek out the odd woman or two my god some were odd too. Catering seemed to attract them as well as the entertainment department. Honestly if the entertainment held a contest for the dirtiest, scruffiest women I new a building full of them" Jodie explained to Faith.

The funniest image was seeing teabags being dried on the washing line, as if there was a shortage, perhaps the foreign tea merchants lost their cargo at sea. My god I wondered what else was going to hang on the line, some things were asking to be pinched. It's funny what happens at these holiday camps plenty of fun for holidaymakers and staff. But no mixing together having relationships with the punters as they are called by the staff. But we did have chalet parties and anyone was invited and virtually anything goes, or so it seems. Faith often cringed when Jodie explained things in her own way, it took a lot to understand Jodie and her unique ways. No wonder Faith got this assignment to watch over her, this was a real test of Faith.

I worked a season in this environment and people began to realise I could sing quite well. I was singing at the karaoke night and the entertainment manager arranged for me to have a personal spot in a show and my own stage show in another theatre. But I was not the type of person who liked fame or popularity; give me the bullying any time, my god not really. It was fun while it lasted and I will treasure the memories there, but I really wanted to go home and be educated. I wanted a career in art and design, or in fashion design demonstrating my artistic flair. Jodie wrote in her diary it would be the last entry for a while as Jodie was determined to get on with her life, without reflecting on her past.

Faith looked on pleased to see me achieve something positive was this the turning point in Jodie's life? At last some good in her pathetic life.

She dreaded the moment when she had to see her parents again; I didn't know how they would respond to me, after all my father wanted me to spend time in jail and pay my debts to society as he put it (Punishment). As she said 'I would love to have seen his face when he discovered that I was innocent'.

Faith read her mind as she made the journey home

"My god, may I say that I was getting more nervous as I got closer to the house, it was strange seeing the old curtains in the windows that I despised so much". She noticed someone peeping from behind the curtains and recognised it to be her father. Suddenly he rushed out the front door; he then stopped and stood in front of me. Jodie looked into his eyes as he looked back at her then looked down in shame. They both stood for a while neither of us saying anything, it was one of them moments that you dread to happen. Finally he gave a cough in order to clear his throat and spoke to Jodie with tears in his eyes.

"I am so sorry Jodie, I feel as if I have let you down" He said his voice was quivering

"Dad I am sorry too, for putting you through absolute hell, but I am heaven blessed and given a second chance" I said sorrowfully.

At that was the moment we embraced and the tears poured like a waterfall, the rest of the family, who had congregated around the door, observed us.

And my god the entire neighbourhood, may god bless the sad bastards who looked on at our reconciliation, a glorious moment never to be repeated.

Faith looked on from afar knowing that Jodie had changed but she still had a long way to go before she could reach perfection.

But Jodie had turned her life around and persevered to do good for others, she had been proven innocent of committing actual bodily harm and she had simply followed the wrong pathway to evil. Faith had shown her the right course and guided her to a brighter future; Jodie was never a really bad girl and just needed showing the right direction into doing good.

INSPIRED SONGS

Who wants to live forever	Queen
Love hurts	Nazareth
Memories	Elvis Presley
Dream	Everly Brothers

GOTH MUSIC
Yummer Yummer man.	Danielle DAX
I walk the line.	Alien sex fiend
Sebastian	Sex gang children.

From the Goth rock ultimate collection

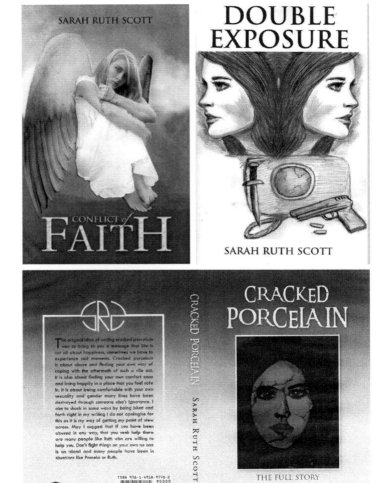

Other books by author to be sent

Lightning Source UK Ltd.
Milton Keynes UK
UKOW03f0734180514

231848UK00001B/12/P